Dr. J. Calvin Alberty's

THE AUDACITY OF BEING A CHRISTIAN

(How could you have thought it was going to be easy?)

Wijah Publishing

WIJAH Publishing Company, LLC

First Edition

wijahpublishing.com

jcalvinalberty.com

All biblical citations are from the King James Version of the Bible unless otherwise noted.
If there are any scriptural quotations marked (NIV,) they are taken from the Holy Bible, New International Version®, NIV®. Copyright © 1973, 1978, 1984, 2011 by Biblica, Inc.™ Used by permission of Zondervan.

"My favorite author," when alluded to, is E. G. White. Unattributed quotations are by Dr. J. Calvin Alberty

ISBN 978-1-940525-22-8
First Edition Printed in the United States of America
Library of Congress Cataloging-in-Publication Data

Alberty, John Calvin
THE AUDACITY OF BEING A CHRISTIAN
(How could you have thought it was going to be easy?)
by Dr. John Alberty. – 1st ed.
Cover image designed by Troy Lyle

About the Author

Dr. Alberty is a Licensed Professional Counselor and an adjunct professor in the state of Georgia. At the time of this publication, he also has the following credentials: Nationally Certified Counselor; Master Addiction Counselor; and Clinically Certified Juvenile Treatment Speicalist. He holds a doctorate (Ed.D.) in Counseling Psychology as well as a Ph.D. in Nutrition from a holistic perspective.

He is passionate about the empowering of others. He believes that there is a time and season for everything under the sun. That time is now for the publishing of "The **Audacity** of Being A Christian." All around us the world testifies of its opposition to God and Christianity. Yet, fewer and fewer have the **AUDACITY** to stand for Christ as believers!

Acknowledgements

Thanks first to God, Who fights my battles. Thanks to my dear wife of more than 45 years (Evelyn). Thanks for her love and devotion to God and family. Her voice is reason. Her smile is food for my spirit. Her laughter is medicine to my soul. Her ways are admirable. Her wisdom is invaluable. Her love is empowering.

I express gratefulness and gratitude to the memory of my mother, Dorothy Bryant, who knew how to love and raise children to love God and others. I believe that her prayers are as powerful today as when they were first uttered to God on behalf of her children and love-ones.

I greatly desire that my two grandsons, John C. Alberty III and Jordan C. Alberty live lives that are Christ-

Centered. I am aware of the future challenges before the both of them. I thank God for the love and competency of their earthly and spiritual parents, John and Kimberli Alberty.

I acknowledge the great influence of my grandmother Elizabeth Davis Bryant. Her love was greatest when I needed it most. This, along with my love for my other sons James, and Corey, motivates me to live a godly life worth emulation. I acknowledge that the most important factor in making this book possible is foreseeing the joy and pleasure of witnessing those empowered by its words as they realize more fully the unity of their transcendent selves with God. Finally, I acknowledge you. As you read this book, my prayer is for you to grow from its inspired content. Thank you for your support.

Dr. J. Calvin Alberty

May you receive a blessing of knowledge that will

enhance and improve your life on this side of His return.

The Author

Dedication

I dedicate this book, "The **Audacity** of Being a Christian: How could you have thought it was going to be easy?" to those who love and study the Word of God. I am speaking of the ones who refuse to entrust their salvation to any man. They employ the wisdom that God has blessed them with to better know Him for themselves. They refuse to be spoon-fed puppets or churchlitically (my word) correct. They rest their salvation on a "THUS SAYS THE LORD."

They have accepted the truth, that all who live godly in Christ Jesus shall suffer persecution. They are therefore ready to lay all on the altar of sacrificial fidelity to God. They will not compromise truth for convenience. They have the unmitigated **AUDACITY** to stand for God in a contemptuous and rebellion filled world.

Dr. J. Calvin Alberty

Warnings and Disclaimers

This text should be used only as a general source of enjoyment and inspiration. This book, and no other book by this author, is intended to replace common sense and wisdom. The purpose of this book is to share with you the powerful possibilities of intentional thinking that yields positive choices and give impetus to good decision-making buttressed by sound reasoning founded in truth.

You are unique, and you must find your own voice. Your voice must be authentic, genuine, and true. You will always find your true voice intimately interwoven with your passions. You must make empowering and life enriching decisions for the enhancement of your future. These decisions will be so stirring, moving, and empowering that they will be heard, felt, and witnessed by others in their observation of the "passionate you."

J. Calvin Alberty, LLC and WIJAH Publishing Company, LLC shall have no liability or responsibility to any person or entity with respect to any loss or damage caused, or alleged to have been caused, directly or indirectly, by the information contained in this book.

This book, "**THE AUDACITY OF BEING A**

CHRISTIAN: How could you have thought it was going

to be easy?" is a book designed to tell its Christian

readers that life will make every effort to injure your

spirit. It will be inflexible and persistent in its effort to

deny you everything that is good or everything that is of

God.

However, you are not to fear life. God is much more

unrelenting in His effort to give you an eternal life of

happiness, than the devil is to take it away. What God

has to offer is immeasurably better and vastly different

than what is found in this dark ether in which we now

coexist. God will not fail in providing His love and

guidance to those who love Him enough to follow His every word. However, it is imperative that we have the courage to trust and obey Him. Do not faint at the threats of the enemy or his recurring assaults against you. Do not become discouraged at the roar of a defeated, toothless, and clawless foe. Trust God with all your heart and soul. He who cannot fail assures that you shall be **victorious!**

THE AUDACITY OF BEING A CHRISTIAN:

How could you have thought it was going to be easy?

BY

DR. J. CALVIN ALBERTY

Dr. J. Calvin Alberty

A FEW EARLY LESSONS THAT LIFE TAUGHT

Jerome was not particularly a bully. In fact, he had been a fairly good guy. The more I think about it, I had never witnessed him in this bullying role before. So why did he choose to be one today? Even more-so, why had he chosen me to be the object of his late-blossoming anger? After all, growing up in the projects of Augusta, Georgia, with a Detroit accent at five years of age, made it tough enough in and of itself. I will get back to Jerome later, but for now, back to an earlier period in my life.

I had very recently turned five years of age. It was a terrible unfolding of events which led to my father's incarceration for domestic violence against a child. That child was me. Maybe it was not the only cause, but it certainly should have been the main cause. How my father had come to such a low point in his life was a very dark and perplexing mystery to me. Perhaps it was his years of consuming or imbibing alcohol, or his military encounters during his tour of duty in the army. It could have even been some dark experiences from a foul and tormented childhood of his own. I am only guessing. The truth is that I do not have a clue what created the man that most called dad, but I called "monster."

However, my not knowing the "why" of what he did, did not obfuscate the fact that something dastardly and austere had caused him to become the vile and violent, antagonist of my formative years. I would discover later what it was, but that revelation is not for this book.

Speaking on the subject of my father, my uncle Calvin Bryant tells the story about giving my father a ride one day. He relates that as they are riding along, my father suddenly demands that my uncle stops his car. Before the car can come to a full stop, my father hastily jumps out of the still moving vehicle. He begins running full speed toward a man standing on the corner of Gwinnett and 9th street. My uncle relates that my father then pulls out his pistol and begins beating this man, into an almost unconscious state, with the butt of his gun. My father then casually walks back to the car, gets inside, and calmly says to my uncle "What are you waiting on? Let's go."

My uncle further recounts that this was not a solitary incident. He states that my father had a history of assaultive behaviors against other men. He initiates his attacks with impunity and very little or no provocation. This was coupled with his having absolutely no remorse, guilt, or compunction for his cruel and brutal acts.

The earliest childhood memories I have of my "so-called" father were his altercations with my mother. They were alcoholic induced, juiced-up emotional outbursts. These outbursts were coalesced with verbal and physical violence toward my mother, which inevitably found its way to me.

Dr. J. Calvin Alberty

My father never struck my other siblings. I cannot recall a single such incident against them. However, he had no issues with striking me. Maybe his aggression was directly related to the fact that I was his only child who would run to bite and fight him each time he assaulted my mother. I was a little more than five years of age. Three of my four siblings were younger than me, which means they were too young to intercede. My older brother, who was seven years of age at that time, for reasons unknown, his responses during those violent outbursts remain detached from my memories. I honestly do not recall his whereabouts, during the first five years of my life. I do recall him calling to my home in my adult life and asking me, "Why did daddy whip you so much?"

There was no rationale that I could supply. The truth is that I did not at that time have a clue, even though the answer had been given to me in ways that I failed to comprehend the obvious.

Regarding my father's violence, it was unique how the characters around his violent eruptions appeared to always be the same. I cannot remember a time when there was an additional character present, or one of the recurring main characters missing. It seems as though every violent event was centered on the triad of my father, my mother, and me.

Allow me to give more details in an effort to contextualize the backdrop. At five years and several months of age, for the first time, I met my father's violence with violence. I do not know where the strength, courage, or perhaps foolishness, had come from, but it had indeed emerged from somewhere within me without being summoned. So, whenever my father would fight my mother, I would run toward him with the sole purpose of biting him as hard as I could somewhere on his upper thigh. I remember being very animated, flailing my arms, and my little five-year-old fists. I tried hard to both punch and bite him. My purpose was specific; to stop or prevent him from hitting my mother.

The fights between my parents escalated until one day I caught a good one in the mouth from my father's fist or from a swift unrighteous back-hand. It all happened so quickly. One moment I was at the kitchen table mean-mugging him for cursing at my mother. The next moment, I was flying backward through the air in what appeared to be in slow motion. I was reaching out and grabbing nothing but air in my effort to grasp onto something to prevent the inevitable impact that I knew awaited me.

Suddenly, the back of my head slammed into the wall somewhere below the kitchen sink. I was literally unconscious. After that, I only remember fading in and out, while being held tightly in my mother's arms. She was running through what must have been several feet of snow. There were multiple large snow mounds, which were common to Detroit's winters. These mounds hampered her progress in distancing herself and me from my angry father.

This day had been filled with a devastating series of woeful and miserable events. As I slowly stirred to an increasing state of consciousness, I awoke to the harsh reality of bitter frigid air blowing forcibly against and pass my face. There was an even more chilling and alarming reality inserting itself into this catastrophic event. There was blood covering my mother's shoulder. I feared that she had been injured more severely than what I initially believed.

Her face was soaked in tears and her shoulder was covered in blood. However, as I began gaining clarity, it hit me harder than the freezing air blowing against my face. The blood on my mother's shoulder represented something even more dastardly than my initial fears.

My mother was desperately laboring through the snow and quite an impossible blast of wind. She was hysterically trudging from one house to another. She was urgently trying to find a neighbor with a phone. All the time she kept looking behind and over her shoulder. It was there, enveloped in that harsh and blistering wintery blast, in a horrifying frozen moment of clarity, that I suddenly realized that the blood on mother's shoulder was my own.

I was bleeding from my nose and mouth. To this day I still remember my mother's desperate and frantic appeals for help. She screamed in desperation with inconsolable tears. Everything occurring was amplified by the frightening and panicky cries from her terrified child. Nothing was more bitter and harsh than the environment through which we were now struggling, except the prospect of once again facing any environment that included my father. My mother's cries had now become deep guttural moans that were muffled by the fierce wind-driven snow. It was a snow and wind that had no conscience. It continued without mercy to assault our faces cruelly, unsympathetically, and incessantly.

I was still a young child when I heard my mother talking to my aunt about the events of that disturbing day. My mother had my father arrested for assaulting both her and me. My Aunt Mary wired my mother the funds needed to leave Detroit that same day. We were on the freedom-train. I would later dub it "The Midnight Train to Georgia," which was an inspiration from Gladys Knight's 1973 hit song.

The events of Detroit had left me with physically indiscernible scars, but emotionally, there were deep and dark long-lasting wounds. As a young child, I was "tie-tongued." At least that is what we called it in the projects of Augusta, Georgia. It simply meant that I struggled in my efforts to speak or formulate sentences. This problem was not about phonics or syntax. It was from being traumatized.

My son, a speech pathologist, would later inform me that my type and onset of stuttering could have been the result of serious traumatic experiences in my childhood. I have revealed these

Dr. J. Calvin Alberty

childhood experiences so that you might gather a deeper understanding of my response to Jerome's threats and other revelations that will be disclosed as you read.

On the day of Jerome's threats to me, I had just finished a Bible study class. It was taught by two elderly white ladies who dared to have the **AUDACITY** to be real Christians. They would come into the inner bowels of the projects and set up their Bible story boards and materials at Ms. Dorothy Briscoe's apartment at 1643 McCauley Street.

These ladies had wooden tripods with felt-boards and felt-type images of biblical characters. On this particular day, I was enthralled in the Bible story about the "Three Hebrew Boys" as were the rest of those in attendance. As the story unfolded, we were told that everyone bowed down to a large golden image that was raised up somewhere in proximity of a place called Babylon. From the perspective of the ladies' teaching, this was a big event. Just about everyone who was anybody was there in compliance with the royal command of King Nebuchadnezzar. In fact, the King himself was there.   The royal musicians were all poised to play music exalting the king. This was not just any music. This music would be the signal announcing that it was time for everyone to bow down to the great and grand golden image that was erected to express the eternal rulership of the King.

Dr. J. Calvin Alberty

Right on cue the music reverberated throughout the crowd, and everyone bowed; well almost everyone bowed. There were these three Hebrew boys to whom the king had been especially kind. These boys did now bow on cue. In fact, they did not bow at all. They seemed not to care about being politically, religious-litically, or church-litically (my daft words) correct. They refused to bow to the newly erected 135-foot-tall gleaming golden image. They refused to do so even though it had been a direct command of the king. This narrative was amazing to me. I was hanging onto every word coming out of their mouths. I hated when the story finally ended. However, it did come to an end, and I immediately started home. It was during this homeward journey that I encountered Jerome.

"Hey boy, where are you coming from?" He demanded of me.

"From Bible studies." I calmly answered.

"Boy, what do you know about Bible studies?" He questioned me in a menacing tone. The expression plastered on his face was one of anger, but how could he be angry at me? I was caught off guard as he added. "Bet you didn't learn a thing."

"I learned that you are not supposed to bow down to anyone but God." I replied in my youthful innocence. It is amazing how the devil takes our own words and uses them against us.

"You're going to bow down to me and you are going to bow down right now or I'm going to knock your head off!" Jerome was now infuriated. He was as mad as that old King Nebuchadnezzar from the Bible story, who was incensed with the three Hebrew boys, Shadrach, Meshach, and Abednego, for not bowing to his image.

"I can't bow down to you Jerome." I replied.

"You will either bow down or get knocked down." He threatened. You have until I count to three and I am going to knock your head off." He began a slow methodical count. "One."

I do not know why, and I cannot even begin to explain it, but I closed my eyes. I then tilted my head and lifted my jaw with my teeth clinched tightly together in preparation for the ensuing assault. I had fought my father and could not understand why fighting Jerome did not come to my mind as an option.

"Two." Jerome shouted in anger.

To this day, I ask myself, why didn't I unleash on him like I had my father? Why did I not run? He could never have caught me. He was about four years older than me, but that is a significant difference when you are only about eight years of age, and the other person is twelve or thirteen. However, I stood there with my jaw and chin prepared for the impact of what would surely be a painful blow. In my child-like contemplations, it dawned on me that the three Hebrew Boys did not fight. This was at least the case in the physical sense. Instead, they depended on God and that is exactly what I was doing unknowingly. I expected God to be with me in this fiery furnace with Jerome.

Suddenly, from nowhere immediately noticeable, urgent, and intense words rang out loudly, "Jerome! Jerome! Come here right now!" It was his grandmother excitedly calling for him with a sense of intense urgency.

I opened my eyes to see his tightly clenched fist frozen in the air above his shoulder and my face. Here is the astonishing thing, that to this day continues to befuddle my mind, his grandmother could not see what was occurring. She was only about ten yards away, but she could not have seen around the corner of her brick apartment to our location. She could not have had the slightest inkling as to what was transpiring. I was in extreme peril and in dire need of immediate help. It was a physical impossibility for her to have any awareness of the effect she was having on my desperate and frightening situation. Yet, she called him as if her house was on fire and he was supposed to bring the water to put it out. "Jerome come here right now!"

Jerome simply looked at me as he lowered his fist and ran away shouting, "I'm going to get you. You'll see!" He quickly ran in the direction of his grandmother's voice. I was just a child, but that event is just as clear in my mind today as if it occurred only moments ago.

Dr. J. Calvin Alberty

Please indulge me for just a moment longer. I must tell you the end of this story. After arriving home, I hid in the house for most of that day. I had that same feeling that would overcome me when I would hide in the closet from my inebriated father. (That is another story). This behavior was a crucial component of my survival mode. This mode automatically activated when he would come home drunk with malevolent and malicious intents.

While hiding out in my bedroom in the projects, my new stepfather, who at the times, I had very little love for, ordered me to go to the store and get him three packs of Pall Mall cigarettes. It was the last thing that I wanted to do. The cigarettes were three packs for a dollar at that time. I wearily took the money from his extended hand and ran as fast as my feet could take me. In no time at all, I had safely reached the store, or so I thought. Just as I reach for the door handle to enter the Curtis' Store, guess who pushed the door open from the other side, to greet my terrified stare?

It was Jerome! He had this big, uncommon smile pasted all over his face. "Hey Calvin. How are you doing?" He said to me as he smiled again and walked away without waiting on an answer. I learned several important lessons on that day. God had not only stopped Jerome from hitting me in my face that day, but He had also given him amnesia. It was blatantly obvious to me that he had forgotten that entire moment and event. He had no remembrance of the blistering and venomous threats that he had made to me only a few hours earlier.

This experience with Jerome cemented in my mind a belief in the protective love and power of an awesome God. It promoted a deeper belief in God for a five-year-old kid desperate to believe that there was a father somewhere that he could believe in and feel loved by.

I embraced this new awareness of a heavenly father. I cherished it before ever possessing a significant understanding of who God was. When this incident is paired with what transpired with my father's brutality, it taught me four simple beliefs from those early lessons in my stressed-out, grievous, and beleaguered young life. The **first** is that "God delivers." **Secondly**, we will always have a need for divine intervention in our lives, even when we do not know it. **Thirdly**, the battles that we encounter in this difficult, grueling, and strenuous thing called life, are not ours. "God will fight His own battles in His own time and in His own way. God's way fully ensures that the needed deliverance becomes an unquestionable reality." **Finally**, "life is hard!" It is even hard for a five-year-old kid in Georgia with a Detroit accent trying to live with the unseen scars left by a man who did not know what he was leaving or doing.

Dr. J. Calvin Alberty

LIFE IS HARD, BEING A CHRISTIAN IS HARDER

In the early classroom of life, I quickly and harshly learned a difficult and lingering lesson from my efforts to escape my father's brutality. It was a clarion call to action from life itself. It taught me these truths that resonated with his every aggressive act. "I was not to allow anyone to define my reality." This particularly rang true with the abuse of my father.

"When it appears that I am helpless, I must ever seek a path that restores a control that moves me toward my goals." "I must adopt and believe the philosophy of "This too will pass, because with God's help, I will make it pass." "I must never become comfortable in an oppressive state of affairs. The acceptance of such a condition is detrimental to anyone's resolve for positive change." "Therefore, I must recognize my limitations, but not believe them. Instead of believing self-imposed limits or those exacted by others, I must find healthy ways to venture beyond them."

"I must ever believe that there is always a way out of mediocracy, normalcy and the average status quo that accepts complacency. There must be a burning desire (passion) to find that path, which is yet to be discovered." "I must know also, that when it appears that there is no way to extract myself from destructive circumstances, or any way to significantly alter my wretched and pitiful condition, I must remember that there is always a way that I am not seeing. It is a way that fear and/or doubt has hidden from me, but it is always there! It is like the sun on an overcast cloudy day or even at night, it is always there. It is a way out that is often deep within you and me called "Passionate Purpose." When Passionate Purpose is coupled with Persistency there are no impenetrable barriers to any goal.

With this understanding, I must remember that a person's purpose, once coupled with their passion and persistency is their ever-present source of pervasive and ubiquitous power. Therefore, the enemy of souls will do everything within his feeble powers to obfuscate, obscure, and confuse us on this very imperative matter. There are three all-encompassing and overarching tenets in every man's life: to **KNOW HIS PURPOSE**, then to

THE **AUDACITY** OF BEING A CHRISTIAN

<u>**PERSISTENTLY LIVE THAT PURPOSE**</u> out <u>**WITH**</u> <u>**PASSION**</u>. He must do this while **ACCEPTING NO** **ALTERNATIVES** to these three vital and essential tenets (**Purpose, Passion, and Persistency**) of his life.

With that said, it was still an extreme and formidable challenge growing up. By age six, I had gathered enough evidence from life to be thoroughly convince that living life is not only hard, but it requires constant and persistent adjustments to overcome its various and innumerable snares and pitfalls.

What was so terrifying about this entire ordeal to me was that life was treating me like this, at such an early age, when I did not want anything in particular from it. I only wanted to be left alone to grow up unmolested by its evil consortium of irritants, spoilers, and players. So, at that early age I concluded that if life was this hard when I did not want anything from it, then how much unbearable would it be if I actually desired something meaningful. The conundrum of life is that you are always in the middle of it. Some feel that death is the only alternative, but in truth, death is never a viable option. Even a five-year-old child knew that.

I read, early in my Christian journey, in **2 Timothy 3:12** "Yea, and all that will live godly in Christ Jesus shall suffer persecution." Well maybe I did not read it. Perhaps I heard some preachers say it. However, I knew immediately, at the very moment of becoming acquainted with this text that those words resonated with me. They told me the truth about life. There was no sugar coating it at all. This journey through life, especially as Christians, would be arduous and daunting at the least.

I knew immediately that I would need help. When I initially consider partnering up with God, there were so many "thou shall nots" that I cringed at even the thought of connecting with God. This was especially the case after life had treated me so disdainfully as a child.

It had jerked me up by the scruff of my neck and shouted, "My name is life! I am a monster. I hate you, you little ....!" Listen to how this is echoed in the Word of God. **John 15:19** reads, "If ye were of the world, the world would love his own: but because ye are not of the world, but I have chosen you out of the world, therefore **THE WORLD HATETH YOU**.

To me, the "world" just meant those people with "life" in them. So, the world and life were chronicled in my young mind as traitorous, low-down, conniving, distrustful people. I never understood that if a Christian's life was supposed to be so difficult, then why did everybody wear fine dresses and suits to church? It seemed as though they should have been dressed in battle fatigues.

It would take me longer to learn that these same people, in the beautiful dresses and suits could smile in your face and plot your demise at the same time. I was told that just because you go into a supermarket does not make you groceries. Just walking into a garage does not make you a car. I was then told, walking in, and sitting down in a church does not make you a Christian.

At the least, this verse of scripture "…**THE WORLD HATETH YOU…**" had identified the enemy. Again, I had enough sense to know that I needed help dealing with such monsters as the "world and life" had to offer.

Do you recognize that you need help?

WELL, DO YOU?

I FINALLY CHOSE GOD AS MY HELPER

I finally chose God as my Helper. He would be my Ally and Friend. I wanted the type of God that the Hebrew Boys and Daniel had. He would be my Savior, LORD, and my God, in a world that hated the both of us. Can you imagine the **AUDACITY** of me choosing God in a world that hates Him and me?

Furthermore, I had the **AUDACITY** to make this choice with intentionality, premeditation, and deliberateness. I had then, and even now, I have the **AUDACITY** to believe that God was and is greater than all my trials, challenges, and prohibiting encounters that life continually launches at me. **1 John 4:4** declares, "Ye are of God, little children, and have **OVERCOME** them: because **greater is he that is in you**, than he that is in the world."

What a blessing and privilege to have God with us. I only wish that I would have decided for him much earlier. However, there was something in my heart so offensive to God that it would take a moment for me to be healed enough to unite with Him. However, I needed Him to help me heal. It was my intense animosity toward my father.

I find comfort and solace in knowing that our God is greater than all our failures, faults and challenges combined. There is no enemy that is within or outside of us that will not eventually bow to Him. **Romans 14:11** certifies, "For it is written, As I live, saith the Lord, **every knee shall bow to me,** and every tongue shall confess to God." This may be hard to conceive by man's measures, but **Jeremiah 32:17** declares, "Ah Lord God! behold, thou hast made the heaven and the earth by thy great power and stretched out arm, and **THERE IS NOTHING TOO HARD FOR THEE**."

So, what does this tell us? It unpretentiously declares that things indeed may be hard, or appear to be too hard for us, but we can rest in the assurance that they are not too hard for God! If God is in you, if you have the **AUDACITY** to claim Him as your own God, then He will fight your every battle. **Deuteronomy 20:3-4** reads, "And shall say unto them, Hear, O Israel, ye approach this day unto battle against your enemies: **let not your hearts**

faint, fear not, and do not tremble, neither be ye

terrified because of them; 4 For **the Lord your**

God is he that goeth with you, **TO FIGHT FOR YOU**

against your enemies, **to save you**." We further find

in **2 Chronicles 20:15** "And he said, Hearken ye, all

Judah, and ye inhabitants of Jerusalem, and thou

king Jehoshaphat, Thus saith the Lord unto you, Be

not afraid nor dismayed by reason of this great

multitude; **FOR THE BATTLE IS NOT YOURS, BUT**

GOD'S. 2 Chronicles 20:17 asserts, "**Ye shall not**

need to fight in this battle: set yourselves, **stand**

ye still, and see the salvation of the Lord with you..."

God cannot fail! With God, we cannot fail!

I have learned this lesson the hard way. That

is to stop trying to fight God's battles! STOP IT!

STOP IT! STOP IT! Our Creator God can defend Himself. He is not a child who whimpers and sobs in the face of adversity. HE IS GOD! What you are presently going through, He has seen a million times. Though it might be unique to you, it is not unique to Him. What frightens us, does not frighten Him. Our God knows no fear. He is all powerful, all knowing, all wise, and very jealous and protective over His children.

He cares more passionately for you than you can ever know. He does not only care about the major storms in our lives. He cares about the splinter in our finger and the sting of a mosquito. This is the very nature of who He is and how He loves. He is

God, and God is Love. Love always protects and keep its blessed recipients safe and secure.

If you have the **AUDACITY** to believe in God, then you should have the **AUDACITY** to believe that He has protection clauses written for you in His Word. **Matthew 18:6** states, "But whoso shall offend one of these little ones **which believe in me**, it were better for him that a millstone were hanged about his neck, and that he were drowned in the depth of the sea." **Psalm 34:7** "The angel of the Lord encampeth round about them that fear him, and delivereth them." **Psalm 91:1-11** "He that dwelleth in the secret place of the most High shall abide under the shadow of the Almighty. 2 I will say of the Lord, He is my refuge and my fortress: my God; in him will I trust. 3 Surely, he shall deliver thee from the snare of the fowler, and from the noisome pestilence. 4 He shall cover thee with his feathers, and under his wings shalt thou trust: his truth shall be thy shield and buckler. 5 Thou shalt not be afraid for the terror by night; nor for the arrow that flieth by day; 6 Nor for the pestilence that walketh in darkness; nor for the destruction that wasteth at noonday. 7 A thousand shall fall at thy side, and ten thousand at thy right hand; but it shall not come nigh thee. 8 Only with thine eyes shalt thou behold and see the reward of the wicked. 9 Because thou hast made the Lord, which is my refuge, even the most High, thy habitation; 10 There shall no evil befall thee, neither shall any plague come nigh thy dwelling. 11 For he shall give his angels charge over thee, to keep thee in all thy ways."

Don't you get it? If you have the **AUDACITY** to call yourself a Christian, then you better have the **AUDACITY** to believe in and stand up for Christ. You must reject the ways and things of this world that would ensnare and fasten you to its luring and destructive trappings and accoutrements.

The reality is that we must know that the devil hates us. The Bible declares emphatically in **Revelation 12:17** The dragon (Satan) was wroth (angry) with the woman (church,) and went to **MAKE WAR** with the remnant of her seed (God's church in the last days), which keep the commandments of God, and have the testimony of Jesus Christ.

So, we have God's word telling us that the devil will be at war with God's church (us), and that all who live godly in Christ Jesus (us) will suffer persecution. So how can we expect for LIFE to be easy? We will shed some tears. We will hurt and suffer loss for His glory. These are the dark circumstances and situations in which we find ourselves while living in a sinful world. Furthermore, when **John 16:33** adds "… **In the world ye shall have tribulation…**" we should be attentive. When we read in **1 Peter 5:8**, "Be sober, be vigilant; because your adversary the devil, as a roaring lion, walketh about, **seeking whom he may devour.**" We should be watchful. Hearing **John 15:19** declare, "If ye were of the world, the world would love his own:

but because ye are not of the world, but I have chosen you out of the world, therefore **THE WORLD HATETH YOU**." This should put us on guard. How could we have ever expected for this mindboggling journey into Christendom to be easy? We are the children of God. We are wandering through a dark and hostile land. Earth in its present form is not our home. We are but sojourners. **Hebrews 13:14** declares, "For here have we no continuing city, but we seek one to come." The Bible declares boldly that we are not of this world, so our hearts should not be rooted in this world or its treasures. **Matthew 6:21** "For where your treasure is, there will your heart be also." This question of clarity must be answered by all. Where is my heart? If our answer is anything other than "in Christ" or "in the activities that will hasten his coming" then we must soberly consider our standing before the Creator of the universe.

This is not to tell you to abandon the world. After all, we live in it. It is also acceptable to amass wealth. However, your energies and resources should be utilized to tell the world about Jesus. In all the confusion, turmoil, and chaos of this world, we find earthly sojourners in search of peace that the world cannot give them. **John 16:33** says, "These things I have spoken unto you, that in me ye might have peace. In the world ye shall have tribulation: but be of good cheer; I have overcome the world. **John 14:27** affirms, "Peace I leave with you, my peace I give unto you: not as the world giveth, give I unto you. Let not your heart be troubled, neither let it be afraid." The world never really gives you peace. It gives you "piece." You know, it gives a **piece** of this or a **piece** of that with a thousand strings of consequences and debts attached. It always has a balance due with an offer of additional credit.

Allow me to close this chapter with these words. Our peace is not in this world. Stop looking for it here. You will be forever disappointed, distressed, and depressed with the "piece" of this world. What so many of us truly long and pine for is the peace of God. The Bible is our apothecary. It has medicine that heals the sin-sick soul. **Philippians 4:7** asserts, "And the peace of God, which passeth all understanding, shall keep your hearts and minds through Christ Jesus." One of the primary reasons that we are so often disheartened and discouraged is because we lose our perspective of what peace is, and where it is truly found. When we look for a source of peace in this world, we are already duped, deceived, and deluded.

If we look anywhere else for this most precious jewel, other than God, then we have already begun to spiral down empty and barren rabbit holes. Are you receiving this solemn and earnest admonition to you? Do not look around you for peace. Look up. Your "redemption," in which you will find peace, is drawing near.

Once you have looked up and invited Christ to fully inhabit your life, you can then look inside of yourself. He will be there, and it is there that you will find that sweet, sweet peace that surpasses all understanding. I repeat the words of **Philippians 4:7,** "And the peace of God, which passeth all understanding, shall keep your hearts and minds through Christ Jesus."

It is important to remember that life is hard in this world, and it becomes even harder when you choose to earnestly live as a Christian. However, the question should never be focused on the level of difficulty to be encountered, or how hard it is living this life. The question should be, "Would it have been worth it?" God gives the answer to this question for every follower of Christ in these few texts. **1 Corinthians 2:9** "But as it is written, Eye hath not seen, nor ear heard, neither have entered into the heart of man the things which God hath prepared for them that love him." **John 14:2** "In my Father's house are many mansions: if it were not so, I would have told you. I go to prepare a place for you." **John 14:3** And if I go and prepare a place for you, I will come again, and receive you unto myself; that where I am, there ye may be also." **Revelation 21:2** "And I John saw the holy city, new Jerusalem, coming down from God out of heaven, prepared as a bride adorned for her husband."

Listen, whatever we might have gone through in this life, on this earth, will seem like nothing when compared to what God, in all his creative genius, has prepared for us after enduring the many and various troubles of this world. **2 Corinthians 4:17** declares, "For our light affliction, which is but for a moment, worketh for us a far more exceeding and eternal weight of glory." We will have the **AUDACITY** to cry aloud in words of glorious excitation…

IT WAS WORTH IT! IT WAS WORTH IT! IT WAS WORTH IT! So, let us cry out even now in faith saying, **IT IS WORTH IT!**

Will you cry out, "It is worth it?

WELL, WILL YOU?

Dr. J. Calvin Alberty

THE AUDACITY OF BEING A GODLY LIABILITY

There is an overwhelming belief that being a liability is, and has always been, a bad thing. People associate the word "liability" with the term "risk." So, the more liable you are, the more at risk you are. The more at risk you are, the more exposed and vulnerable you are. The more exposed and vulnerable you are, the greater the likelihood of personal or corporate injury.

However, upon a closer investigation of this scenario, specifically from a Christian's perspective, vulnerability by the world's terms, is not the same as vulnerability by God's terms. In the world we ask, "Why should we allow ourselves to be exposed and therefore vulnerable?" Why incur risks that can result in personal or corporate injuries or damages? In assuming this posture, we may mitigate or even alleviate worldly disputations, conflicts, or hardships. However, it is not so with the work given to those who are appointed to the mission of building the kingdom of God.

God's counsel to us in "**Matthew 10:16** is, "Behold, I send you forth as sheep in the midst of wolves: be ye therefore wise as serpents, and harmless as doves." Is the call to accomplish this mission not a true liability? Do we grasp the deeper essence of what this is saying? Do we see the picture painted by God? Sheep are always vulnerable to the wolves, or "lions and tigers and bears, oh my!" God tells us this because He will not have us ignorant or unaware to our exposure to the danger of being a Christian. He will not have His church in any situation where they lack wisdom or knowledge about those who are in opposition to the followers of the Most-High God.

Yet, this setting of "sheep and wolves" is one that is both a cautionary and instructive tale. As sheep, according to **Proverbs 3:5**, we are to "Trust in the Lord with all thine heart; and lean not unto thine own understanding." Wolves are an intelligent, cunning, and purpose-driven team of predators. If they do not kill, then they do not eat. If they do not eat, then they do not survive. They are not wholly committed to destroying sheep. However, they are also fully committed to their own survival. Sheep are

THE **AUDACITY** OF BEING A CHRISTIAN

but a means to that end. However, sheep see the wolves' "means to an end" as a dreadful liability to themselves. Their peace rests in one fact. They know that the Good Shepherd is ever near and is always attentively watchful.

By all observable worldly measurements, the Hebrew boys increased their exposure and therefore their risk to harm when they refused to follow the commands of King Nebuchadnezzar. The Bible states that because of their defiance to the king's command, they were ordered to be thrown into a fiery furnace heated seven times hotter than normal.

If you were a company or corporation that was represented by the Hebrew boys, would you oust or fire them? Would you minimize your risk and exposure to the politically correct world and rid yourself of their sort? How about Daniel, who would not stop praying to God, because praying was not the politically correct thing to do, would you fire him also?

There is a decision to be made. You are the corporate official responsible for making the decision to rid your organization of Daniel and the Hebrew boys. You cannot straddle the fence now. How must you make the decision? Will you base your actions on what is best for the corporation in the "here and now" or what best glorifies God, here, now, and forevermore?

The truth is this. you cannot stop corporate officials from making decisions that are based on their bottom-line results. Businesses are not the same. Employees used to matter a whole lot more, but now the emphasis is profit. Corporate officials will make choices based on their corporate interests. They must answer to their board of directors, who in turn must answer to their stockholders. Profit and loss statements identify what they keep or rid themselves of. It is not personal. It is business.

The point being made is that you are not a corporation. Your decisions are personal. Your bottom line is God or Satan. Your loss is heaven. Your gain is eternal life. Your decisions are always based on two factors, love for God, and love for your fellow man. It is not about whether you would fire Daniel or the Hebrew boys. It is about you as a

Christian. Will you seek politically correctness? Will you seek what is best for the corporation Y-O-U, or the building of the kingdom or our eternal G-O-D? Anything other than standing for God will equate to firing Daniel and the Hebrew Boys. The Hebrew boys watched all before them bowing to a golden image. Noah saw the whole antediluvian world renounce God's plea to them. Yet, God's servants did their part. They could not sway the attitudes of those around them, but they did their part in personally standing for God.

You can always do your part in personally standing for God. This stand must be taken with a "No Matter What" attitude.

However, in this world, the "No Matter What" posture, in regard to your love for God, can come with severe earthly consequences in this ether of gloom and darkness. So, what it boils down to is, "Who will you trust and obey?"

Psalm 56:11 tells us, "In God have I put my trust: I will not be afraid what man can do unto me." This text of scripture lets me know that the devil, working through man, will surely attack you when you place your trust in God. I go back to my earlier question, "What? Did you think that it would be easy serving God in a world that hates Him and His followers?"

Listen, the attacks will certainly come. Your trust must unconditionally be in God. There is no other defense. As you are bombarded, you must put on the whole armor of God. Concomitantly, you must declare in your agony and pain, and in the presence of your attackers, who are gloating and feeling victorious. While you acknowledge your pain, also trumpet the end game. Shout hallelujah about how it all turns out. The end game is found in the words of **Romans 8:28** "And we know that all things work together for good to them that love God, to them who are the called according to his **purpose**." There is that word again! I repeat that your **purpose with passion and persistency (Three P's)** is your insurmountable and insuperable power. However, your Three P's must be in harmony with God's goal for your life. When they are lined up with God's goal, it shows that you have placed your trust in Him.

For this reason, King David cries out in **Psalm 16:1** "Preserve me, O God: for in thee do I put my trust." **Psalm 18:2** "The Lord is my rock, and my fortress, and my deliverer; my God, my strength, in whom I will trust; my buckler, and the horn of my salvation, and my high tower." **Psalm 56:4**, "In God I will praise his word, in God I have put my trust; **I will not fear what flesh can do unto me**."

Yes, the attacks will come when you work in any setting (Corporate or otherwise) where you seek to promote the cause of God. This is not about achieving some great, magnanimous, or conspicuous feat or exploit. These attacks will come because of your quiet, ethical, and principled Christian lifestyle. The enemy of souls will show up and he will be prepared to show out.

Do not be alarmed when the devil does his job. It is what he is supposed to do. As my son says, "It is what it is." You should be at peace knowing that our great and formidable God will show up too. He will defend you. He will guide you. He will shelter and protect you. You must not trust your ears or your eyes! You cannot faint because of what you hear and see. Your trust must be in His Word! You must not trust your history, or what has happened before! You must fully trust in every word that proceeds out of the Mouth of God! You must not trust your feelings! You must trust His Word! When all things around you appear to be falling apart, you must still trust His Word!

You may appear to be a liability to the world, but you are seen by God as a reliability for His church. The world's liability is God's reliability. Never forget the experiences of Job. When trouble is all around you, imagine that God is asking the same question he asked of Satan concerning Job in Job 1:8. "And the Lord said unto Satan, Hast thou considered my servant Job, that there is none like him in the earth, a perfect and an upright man, one that feareth God, and escheweth evil?"

Maybe in our trials, our God is serving us up as an example worthy of emulation. Never forget the words in **Luke 1:37,** "For with God nothing shall be impossible." Job was nothing by himself. The Bible is clear in **John 15:5** where Jesus states, "I am the vine, ye are the branches: He that abideth in me, and I in him, the same bringeth forth much fruit: for without me ye can do nothing." This was the formula of success for Job, Daniel, and the Hebrew boys. Before it was ever written in **Philippians 4:13,** they knew these words in their hearts, "I can do all things through Christ which strengtheneth me."

We must realize that God never gives His followers more than they can bear. However, apart from God we can do nothing. Job strength was never in or of himself. It was in the God that he served.

Samson found this out the hard way, as I have also done in too many instances. He thought that he was strong in and of himself, but when he disobeyed God's command, he found that he was not. God left him, but God did not entirely give up on him. Praise God for that! The Bible says in **Judges 16:20** "And she said, The Philistines be upon thee, Samson. And he awoke out of his sleep, and said, I will go out as at other times before, and shake myself. And he wist (knew) not that the Lord was departed from him." God's Spirit had left him, and he did not even know it.

Hear this one additional point. With God we can do everything, and without Him we can do nothing. If the world views you as a liability when you are teamed up with God, it does not matter. What does matter is that there are no more impossibilities in your life with God. Despite how insurmountable your obstacles might appear, never forget **Isaiah 54:17**, "No weapon that is formed against thee shall prosper; and every tongue that shall rise against thee in judgment thou shalt condemn. This is the heritage of the servants of the Lord, and their righteousness is of me, saith the Lord."

Will you believe God and trust that no weapon formed against you will prosper? Will you have the **AUDACITY** to believe that with God you can do all things? Will you accept that all things are possible with God? Will you hear the world calling you a liability and be at peace knowing that God's view of you is vastly different? Will you deafen your ears to all the critics who are comfortably wrapped in their subjective opinions as they judge you unworthy, ill informed, sold out to the enemy of souls, and contrary to the views of the majority? Will you accept their views though they have as much strength as ropes of sand? Will you kowtow, surrender, concede, or yield to their distorted views?

Will you accept and do these things at their urgings?

WELL, WILL YOU?

AUDACITY IN A REAL-WORLD SETTING

A young man commits himself to service for God. He is a simple, honest, and beloved young man. He has a great love for God. It is a love that is married to his fondness for teaching children. His priorities are clear. He teaches and encourages them to be respectful to others, while respecting themselves. He focuses on the value of each child and inspires them to value themselves. He is adamant that they learn about the things of the temporal world, but he asserts even more that they pursue a knowledge and understanding of things eternal.

Like the biblical character Joseph, all that he touches prospers. He is elevated to a position of leadership. This is followed by other successive unsought promotions.

Like Joseph, this God fearing professional never actively sought any positions in the upper echelons of his specialty. God had given him a spirit where he did not believe in politicking or going in round-a-bout circuitous ways to gain advantages over others. He is straight forward with a motto of, "Give your best in making others their best." When he is paid compliment by others, he quickly directs all glory to God.

Then it happens. The promotion of a lifetime is offered with generous benefits. He prays for directions and is convinced that this door has been opened for him by God. He purposes to be a blessing to those that God places in his sphere of influence. He takes the position. His immediate goal is to increase the performance ratings of all employees by speaking with them and listening to their concerns and needs.

He wants to know their **purpose** and **passion**, and if they believe enough in both to be **persistent**. He wants to hear and act on their views of creating a more positive culture in the realm of education. His goal is to fan the flames of unity that will empower leaders, staff, and students.

He is focused on the structuring and implementation of a shared vision. It is a vision that will be to the glory of God and the good of men. He is so focused that he does not sense or detect the evil underhanded, devious groundwork being laid by the past ousted administration.

The adversaries lay a dark foundation teeming with half-truths and outright lies. He could have called them out for what they were. He could have fought in the flesh and spewed counter allegations. However, he willfully allowed his hands to be tied. He could use none of the profane, coarse, odious, and foul weapons of his accusers. He chose instead to don the armor of humility and faith in God. He thought daily on how he must govern himself by meditating on a text of scripture that had often encouraged him in his most challenging times. He had personalized the first part of **2 Corinthians 5:14** For the love of Christ constraineth me…

Nonetheless, he was devastated. He was overwhelmed, not with the audaciousness of his accusers and antagonists, but who his antagonists were. He thought and believed that they were of the ilk and character that he imagined was the foundation of all Christian brothers and sisters. These were not enemies outside the gates. These were wolves in sheep clothing. This had really caught him off-guard. He had made sure that the doors were bolted and locked. He had doubled checked the windows. He had set the house alarm to instant. Yet, despite all the precautions taken, he was attacked in a manner that he never saw coming.

It was the singularity of his thinking that had left him exposed, vulnerable and at risk, in a bad sort of way. He thought that the enemy, if he ever would come, would come from the outside. He never considered, even for a moment, that the enemy was already firmly situated in the figurative house with him. Not only was the enemy there in the house, but he had been there for a while.

This particular enemy possessed one of the most beautiful and disarming smiles imaginable. He spoke glibly with smooth, soft, and kind words. Nevertheless, these things were only tools designed and employed to do a job. They were to create illusions of authenticity that were only ephemeral and transient disguises. They were disguises that had effectively camouflaged the wolves and veiled their dark and angry motives. They were fully cloaked wolves who had calculated and well concealed their foul, obscene, and abominable motives.

How masterfully and flawlessly they masqueraded about while hiding their truly caustic and corrosive intents. It was a nefarious and despicable evil. It was an evil that silently and stealthily wove its web of treachery and deceit. It did this while its sneers and smirks paraded themselves as earnest and sincere smiles.

He never saw it coming. It was so imperceptible and smooth until even after it ran him over, he was still trying to figure out what happened. He checked and rechecked every door and window. He even checked the fireplace. It was only then that he began checking those that appeared as angels of light and conducted themselves as innocent and harmless sheep. Through the fine cracks in their shiny armor, he was now beginning to see that they were rapacious, and ravenous wolves.

They were so good at their deceptions until even they believed themselves to be sheep. When they stood in front of their mirrors, they did not give attention to their long bloody fangs. They did not hear the growling, howling, and snarling that emanated from their drooling lips. Their long-pointed ears were to them nothing more than uncurled fleece.

Wolves in sheep clothing are often invisible to sheep, that is until the wolves are injured. The wolves' injuries cause them to cry aloud in the only voice they have. It is the growling and howling of wolves. When the sheep raise their heads to locate the source of this sound, they only see sheep. Normally, they would never see or hear the wolf until it was too late. This subtleness is the wolves' area of expertise. Imperceptible and insidious subterfuge is instinctive to the wolf. The sheep's only hope is the proximity of the Good Shepherd.

In the case of this amazing educator, the Shepherd stepped in and fought the battle for him. Please note, that the Good Shepherd also gave him his part to do. He was to fight only with the tools of Christians. They were tools such as love, prayer (even for his enemies), commitment to godly principles, and faith in God. He was not to speak evil of anyone or touch any weapon not of God. However, God would touch the hearts of those who were able to make a positive difference in his situation. God not only fought his battle, but covered him with hands of mercy and grace as the storm was passing over.

This is what God will do for any of us who would dare have the **AUDACITY** to trust in Him and His way. This especially includes those followers of Christ, who clearly understand that it is in their weakness that God is strongest. It is not by their strength, but by God's Spirit that victory is wrought. **Zechariah 4:6** declares, "Then he answered and spake unto me, saying, This is the word of the Lord unto Zerubbabel, saying, Not by might, nor by power, but by my spirit, saith the Lord of hosts." This young educator, in the eyes of the wolves, had the **AUDACITY** to make himself vulnerable, to make himself a liability by trusting that God's way was the only way to deal with his enemies. The wolves laughed, but they would not have the last laugh.

How about you? Have you ever wanted to run ahead of God and take matters into your own hands? This may have especially been the case when all around you seemed to be falling apart. Remember these texts of scripture, **Isaiah 40:31,** "But they that wait upon the Lord shall renew their strength; they shall mount up with wings as eagles; they shall run, and not be weary; and they shall walk, and not faint." **Psalm 27:14**, "Wait on the Lord: be of good courage, and he shall strengthen thine heart: wait, I say, on the Lord." **Psalm 37:9** "For evildoers shall be cut off: but those that wait upon the Lord, they shall inherit the earth." **Proverbs 20:22,** "Say not thou, I will recompense evil; but wait on the Lord, and he shall save thee."

Do you have the **AUDACITY** to be a Christian? I am asking, do you have the **AUDACITY** to be a Christian, not just in fair weather conditions, but in the gale storms of life? Paul found himself in a ship being tossed to and fro on a most tempestuous sea. When everyone was ready to jump overboard, Paul made a simple statement found in **Acts 27:31**, "Paul said to the centurion and to the soldiers, Except these abide in the ship, ye cannot be saved."

I ask again, do you have the **AUDACITY** to abide in the ship as a Christian during the foul storms of this life? Do you have the **AUDACITY** and courage to stay in the ship when all of those around you are shouting "Jump!" Do you have the **AUDACITY** and courage to wait upon the Lord and allow Him to fight your battles His way? His way may be the sound of silence while your name and reputation is being dragged through the mud. Do you have the AUDACITY to wait on Him and let Him fight your battles?

WELL, DO YOU?

THE AUDACITY OF CHRISTIANS TO IGNORE THE STATS

There are statistical configurations and permutations that are designed to consider every known variable or influence. Yet, my initial introduction to statistics was as an undergraduate student in a "Probability and Statistics" class. On that first night the professor, who was from the math department, declared there is a lie, a darn lie, and then there are statistics. He went on to demonstrate how, when measurements of central tendency are manipulated, we can use the same raw data to arrive at multiple and varying statistical outcomes.

Statistical research might yield thousands of reasons for us to take a certain path in life. Right now, in this world we are admonished to reject the biblical accounts or narratives of creation and instead, we are invited to adopt theories of evolution created by Charles Darwin and others. Their multifaceted statistical approaches are identified and claimed as the absolute declarations of truth and facts. The insurmountable and unassailable truth is that their declarations of certitude are only unfounded, unsubstantiated, and hypothetical theories.

Yes, the enemy of souls desires to paint the biblical representation of creation and other scriptural topics as false theories. On the other hand, they want to paint the Darwinist theories as pure and flawless intractable facts. Many take their foolish choices and label them as knowledge when they are anything but that. This is not a light or trivial matter. What we believe on earth is central to who we profess ourselves to be as Christians.

It is alarming to me that most people do not connect what they choose to believe to their eternal destinations, or their forever home, or what is best known as heaven. "Choices are destination!" We simply must not be deceived in this vitally important area by the yowls, yelps, and yaps of the majority. God is never defined or confined by the limited knowledge of man, nor is His wisdom and knowledge subject to finite brains.

His boundlessness is inexplicable. It cannot be grasped or comprehended with the deepest of cogitations. It cannot be debated to an end even with the most profound and astute deliberations. God's knowledge is truly an unfathomable unknown. What man knows of Him is only that which our awesome God has revealed. His wisdom dwells in a barely explored bottomless well of impenetrable permutations, variations, and forms.

There is no Euler's identity formula to identify the extremes of God. There is no String theory, which is a "theory of everything," that can explain God. He is vaster than the entire expanse of the known and unknown universe. There are no eternal cogitations by man that can adequately quantify, codify, or demystify the Sovereign of all life and everything. He is God! Humanity cannot even begin to broach or approach what God has not revealed, even with their most brilliant and sagacious minds.

As Christians, our faith is our facts. We cannot wrap statistics around what we know God to be. This is a point that we must be able to unapologetically articulate, even if it is only to ourselves. It is alright not to be able to fully explain Him, or reduce Him, and his powers to statistics and theories.

I mean, how do you feed thousands with five loaves of bread and two fish? How do you walk on water? How do you come from a tomb after being dead for three day or raise someone from the dead who has been deceased for four days? How does the hem of His garment make healthy that which has been diseased for twelve years? How does He command the wind, rain, and waves to be still, and they obey? How does a virgin give birth to a baby without man's assistance? How do you blow horns and massive walls come tumbling down? How do you walk through the Red Sea on dry land? How? How? How? Do not ask me **how** He did it. All I know is **that** He did.

GOD IS OUR "HOW!"

WE MUST NEVER BE EMBARRASSED BY THE GOSPEL!

Statistics say that if it cannot be figured out, if it does not have a cause-and-effect relationship, if there is no positive or negative correlation, if it cannot be reduced to a formula, or heard, touched, seen, smelled, or tasted, then it did not happen and does not exist. It is deemed as totally irrelevant poppycock. However, we as Christians are blessed to know better and have the **AUDACITY** to articulate our convictions. We place God above statistics and every foolish theory that is paraded as facts with intentions of contradicting the Word of God.

So why does the enemy bombards us continuously, in this life, with shameless lies presented as the pure unadulterated truth? He does so because of the gullibility and the pervasiveness of the herd mindset. It is not that people are illiterate, it is just that most of them are fact-lazy.

Those of authority in this world, knows that if they say something often enough, it will soon resonate as truth to the fact-lazy inhabitants of this planet. They think that because the majority is doing it or advocating for it to be done, then it must be the right thing to do. They forget the examples of the antediluvian world during Noah's days, or many erroneous religious leaders during Jesus' day, or the inhabitants of Sodom and Gomorrah, or even the priests of Baal at Mount Carmel, and others.

There are also scriptural affirmations in **Matthew 7:13-14** that speak against blindly following the majority. It states, "Enter ye in at the strait gate: for wide is the gate, and broad is the way, that leadeth to destruction, and **many** there be which go in thereat: 14 Because strait is the gate, and narrow is the way, which leadeth unto life, and **few** there be that find it." **Matthew 15:14** says, "Let them alone:

they be blind leaders of the blind. And if the blind lead the blind, both shall fall into the ditch."

We live in a time when men willfully ignore God's stats and wisdom, while embracing the foolishness of imperfect, fallible scientists that once wore diapers as babies. The problem is that they spend too much time studying the creation and not time studying the Creator. They believe the stats and theories of this world and then laugh at Christians for having the **AUDACITY** to believe in God and His incalculable statistics on the power of His love for humanity.

They fail to compute the power of His blood to cleanse us from all sin. None-believers are amazed and disturbed at our **AUDACITY** to believe our God who is truth. Yet they have no problem believing lies spawned by the one who is a liar and the father of a lie (Satan). Now figuring out why they do not believe God while believing the devil is truly a study for all eternity.

Will you have the Audacity to tell challengers of the gospel that you do not know everything, but God does. Can you tell them that you cannot explain all of what you believe, but one day God will? Will you tell them that you are not ashamed of the Gospel of Jesus Christ? Will you have the **AUDACITY** to tell that to them?

WELL, WILL YOU?

THE AUDACITY OF THE LYING ENEMY

Let us consider for a moment the deep thralls of darkness in which King David found himself. How do you think he felt as he uttered these words in **Psalm 38:6?** "I am troubled; I am bowed down greatly; I go mourning all the day long." **Psalm 38:12** "They also that seek after my life lay snares for me: and they that seek my hurt speak mischievous things, and imagine deceits all the day long." **Psalm 44:22** "Yea, for thy sake are we killed all the day long; we are counted as sheep for the slaughter." **Psalm 73:14** "For all the day long have I been plagued, and chastened every morning."

Also, consider Jeremiah when he cried out in **Jeremiah 9:1** "Oh that my head were waters, and mine eyes a fountain of tears, that I might weep day and night for the slain of the daughter of my people!" **Jeremiah 31:15** "Thus saith the Lord; A voice was heard in Ramah, lamentation, and bitter weeping; Rachel weeping for her children refused to be comforted for her children, because they were not."

These men could have reached these low points for many reasons. Maybe it was their recognition of their own sad conditions. It could have been because of the unrepentant state of God's people. I know that in my personal case, it has at times been my own languishing faith when God did not answer my prayers in the affirmative.

There were issues and feelings of abandonment when my own sins rose up to remind me that I was not worthy to be heard by God. Often, this was due to a history of disobedience. It caused me to seriously doubt my worthiness to have my prayers answered.

However, as I matured as a Christian, I finally understood that through my deeds, I would never be, and could never be worthy of having my prayers heard, less more than answered in the affirmative by God. Even the foolish concept of my perceived goodness was explained by Isaiah as he wrote in **Isaiah 64:6** "But we are all as an unclean thing, and **<u>ALL</u> our righteousnesses are as filthy rags**; and we all do fade as a leaf; and our iniquities, like the wind, have taken us away."

I was so relieved to find out that God does not depend on my goodness. This was especially comforting and uplifting after I discovered that I **HAD** no righteousness of my own. It was a great relief to find that God depends only upon the blood of Jesus when it comes to the salvation of my, or anyone else's soul. I do not know about most people, but I am good with that! I am good with realizing that my attempt, to dare and try to merit something from God for my good deeds, is craziness on my part. In fact, I cry out, "Oh Lord, what a load lifted from my shoulders." It is a load that I was incapable of shouldering. I was so happy to read in **1 Peter 5:7** "Casting all your care upon him; for he careth for you."

Satan was trying to get me to focus on doing the impossible, meriting grace. For me, it was a situation of continual failure. I would try to live a perfect life in my own strength. I failed miserably each and every time. Finally, I gave it to God. I cried "Lord, I am so tired of breaking promises to you. I am so tired that I am almost ashamed to get on my knees and bow before you to pray. Help me God to surrender everything to you. Implement Your plans for my life. My plans are flawed, unachievable, and they are unknowingly creating snares from which I cannot escape.

It is wonderful that our God is merciful. I am still a work in progress, but I honestly thank God, that today is so much better than yesterday. I am no longer dependent upon myself. I am, totally, and completely dependent on God. I would have it no other way. As He holds me in His hands, I hear these words from **John 10:28** "And I give unto them eternal life; and they shall never perish, neither shall any man pluck them out of my hand." Did you hear that? I cannot earn it because He says that he GIVES eternal life to us. We cannot earn it!

My own plans caused me to doubt God. They were constructed by this foolish man with ideas and methodologies that were not found in the Bible. The doubts that they created were the works of Satan. There is one thing that I have come to know for sure. There is no room for doubt in the Christian experience.

The enemy uses doubt to weaken us. He wants us to question the love and power of God. Doubt is designed to destroy our experience with God, our belief and faith in God, and our trust and belief in His promises. Alexandre Dumas is quoted as saying, "A person who doubts himself is like a man who would enlist in the ranks of his enemies and bear arms against himself. He makes his failure certain by himself being the first person to be convinced of it" (brainyquote.com). I modified this quote to say, "When a man doubts himself, he is doomed to failure. For his doubt has placed him as a conspirator with the very ones that oppose him. He is sure to lose his battle, for now one is in the ranks of the enemy who knows his every fear and weakness."

Doubt brings fear. **Deuteronomy 28:66** states, "And thy life shall hang in doubt before thee; and **thou shalt fear day and night**, and shalt have none assurance of thy life:" Doubt will sap away your power and will cause you to sink deeply into despair and depression. Think about the time when Peter was walking on the water. He took his eyes from Jesus for only a moment, and he began sinking. **Matthew 14:31** says, "And immediately Jesus stretched forth his hand, and caught him, and said unto him, O thou of little faith, **wherefore didst thou doubt?**" **Matthew 21:21** "Jesus answered and said unto them, Verily I say unto you, If ye have faith, **and doubt not,** ye shall not only do this which is done to the fig tree, but also if ye shall say unto this mountain, Be thou removed, and be thou cast into the sea; it shall be done." **Mark 11:23** "For verily I say unto you, That whosoever shall say unto this mountain, Be thou removed, and be thou cast into the sea; **and shall not doubt in his heart**, but shall believe that those things which he saith shall come to pass; he shall have whatsoever he saith."

Doubt causes us to be unsure, which leads to instability. Doubt causes us to think one way one moment and another way the next moment, as if we were double minded. **James 1:8** says, "A double minded man is unstable in all his ways."

A little doubt is like a little yeast or leaven. **Galatians 5:9** says that "A little leaven leaveneth the whole lump." Satan knows that just a little doubt will have a serious impact upon the entire man. So why does the enemy have the **AUDACITY** to boldly lie? It is simple. His goal is to get us to doubt God. He knows that if we lack confidence in God, we become fearful. This accentuates the enemy's secondary purpose; to instill fear in us. Now put these two traits together: to be doubtful and fearful of God.

If the enemy is successful in both attacks, he has an unstable man or woman who is to be tossed back and forth and anyway the wind blows. So, this is why the devil has the **AUDACITY** to continually tell the same old lies. There is nothing new under the sun. The devil just repackages his lies in new wrappings with more radiant and glittering bows. Why is he so **audacious** and bold? The answer is simple. What he is doing is working. His past success keeps him on the same course. He must be somewhere singing songs about the predictability and gullibility of human beings.

Such successes by the enemy can only prevail when people do not love the truth. God says in **2 Thessalonians 2:10-12,** "And with all deceivableness of unrighteousness in them that perish; because **they received not the love of the truth,** that they might be saved. 11 And for this cause God shall send them strong delusion, that they should believe a lie: 12 That they all might be damned who believed not the truth, but had pleasure in unrighteousness." The ignorance of **lazy-fact** people, who are delusional because they love not the truth continues to fuel the **AUDACITY** of the enemy.

Ask yourself this question and then answer it as honestly and as earnestly as you can. Am I an embracer of truth? Do I love truth, or do I love what my pastor says? Do I love truth or my family's traditions? Do I love truth! Do I love truth? Do I love truth?

WELL, DO YOU?

THE AUDACITY TO STAND AND ENDURE

2 Timothy 3:12 proclaims, "Yea, and all that will live godly in Christ Jesus shall suffer persecution." In considering this text of scripture, why become a Christian in the first place? I mean, who wants to be persecuted? This is telling us as explicitly as possible that the storm clouds are gathering. When you consider that the only staying or arresting power of these volatile and turbulent forces on earth now, is God. He alone, because of His immense love, is keeping this persecutory global tsunami from breaking loose upon us. Without His restraining love, Christianity would be overwhelmed by the dark powers, to which has been given limited control, of this world. On this subject, the Bible is not silent.

We read in **Revelation 7:1,** "And after these things I saw four angels standing on the four corners of the earth, holding the four winds of the earth, that the wind should not blow on the earth, nor on the sea, nor on any tree." Those who study the Bible are acutely aware of the fact that these winds will soon be released. They are the destructive and punishing winds of turmoil, mayhem, strife, and confusion.

At this very moment God's Spirit is working in harmony with these angels to give as many people as possible a chance to decide for Christ. However, the Word of God has announced in **Genesis 6:3,** "And the Lord said, My spirit shall not always strive

114

with man, for that he also is flesh: yet his days shall be an hundred and twenty years."

God has waited patiently for the family of man to abandon its wicked ways and embrace His love and truth. He gave the people of Noah's day 120 years to repent of their evil. God now warns us in **Genesis 6:3** that the restraint of these destructive forces will soon end with unparallel devastation being the result.

John 9:4 is clear in making us aware that time is running out before worldwide persecution against believers is an active and present reality. This will be an event that is so great that we will only be able to live for and wait on Christ in small groups of believers. It will be as it were in the time of the early

Christian Church, or at the times of the Waldenses, or others who dared to stand for God as storm clouds of anger and rage burst open upon them. Yet, still they were faithful. A faithfulness found in such men as John Wycliffe, Huss and Jerome, Martin Luther, and others faithful souls who are never to be named in this present life.

John 9:4 reads, "I must work the works of him that sent me, while it is day: **the night cometh, when no man can work.**" Do you hear what the Word of God is saying? There is coming a time that no man can work to change the hearts of evil men. Every believer will be sealed for God, and every nonbeliever will be sealed for destruction.

Just as Satan, Judas, and the entire antediluvian world crossed lines for which salvation was no longer available, so it is in our present world. It is brazenly and unapologetically marching down similar paths of "no return." When we consider the last days of earth's history and the spiritual decline of humanity, we should easily be able to discern that the constraining Spirit of God is being withdrawn from the earth. **2 Timothy 3:13** offers this truth, "But evil men and seducers shall wax worse and worse, deceiving, and being deceived."

As you look around, are you noticing that morally things **are** not getting better? In fact, are you alert to the reality that they are doing exactly what the Bible predicted? They are getting worse and worse. Do you see and perceive how much more demonically filled and evil man is becoming as God's Spirit is slowly being withdrawn from the earth?

As the four winds are being released, the unavoidable truth of the catastrophic consequences is clearly manifesting itself. The truth that this is leading to is harsh and simple. It is becoming as it was in the days of Noah. We know what happened in Noah's day, don't we? Listen to this description given in **Genesis 6:5,** "And God saw that the wickedness of man was great in the earth, and that **every imagination** of the **thoughts** of his heart was **only evil continually**." Listen to these words. Man was so evil that every imagination of his thoughts was evil, and his thoughts were evil **continually!** How will we as Christians, as trumpeters of truth for God possess the **AUDACITY** as faithful believers of God to stand up to this type of persecution? Think about it. When the going gets rougher, why would anyone stand and be persecuted, when all they would have to do is abandon the cause of God? When the billows of tyranny and a one-world order roll over the entire earth will you stand? When the tempest of global domination, by demonically possessed despots, tosses us here and yonder, will you stand? Will you stand, or will you run for the hills and abandon the Old Ship of Zion and every one of your once sacred Christian values?

After all, isn't It much easier to kowtow and bow to our fears and corrupt peers as we are embroidered and affixed with the labels "fair-weather Christians" and "hypocrites?" Go ahead, the devil says, and stop building on God's kingdom of light. Why put up with all the hassle and persecution. Who will even notice? You can just walk away. I mean nobody told you that it would be this hard building God's church, he whispers. Go ahead quit, make me and my imps a happy lot. Pack up and take your skills, talents, and God-given gifts away with you.

Yes, even though God used you to quadruple church-school enrollment in only a few short years, QUIT! Even though your life-lived and your testimonies have inspired thousands; go ahead and quit, even though you said that you would never turn around. Go ahead and quit; even though God has laid His mighty hand upon you. Go ahead and quit, even though He has elevated you in stature and in the minds and hearts of men so that you could influence them greatly for His cause. Go on about your earthly business and walk away.

Walk away, even though the Great God of Creation has so much more in store for you to do. Go ahead and quit. These are the words of admonition and admonishment from the devil's simpering lips and lying tongue. These are the discouraging and dispiriting shrieks, squeals, and squawks of this old conniving, scheming, and powerless liar. In his defeated state he is outrageously and intensely angry with you.

During this horrid and frightening time that is too soon to come in earth's not so distant future, how will you have the boldness and **AUDACITY** to stand for Christ? Maybe you will not have the tenacity after all. Maybe you will recant, renounce, and disavow your faith in God and the truths that you had so adamantly held sacred. Do you realize that there has never been a time of destructiveness, like that which is to come upon this earth since time immemorial? Never! Not ever!

This will be a most unimaginably difficult time. It will be like the time which Jeremiah calls "the time of Jacob's trouble." **Jeremiah 30:7** professes, "Alas! for that day is great, so that **none is like it**: it is even

THE **AUDACITY** OF BEING A CHRISTIAN

the time of Jacob's trouble, but he shall be saved out of it."

Does this frighten you? What did you think? Did you think it would be easy? Ask yourself, was it easy for Peter, James, or John? Was it easy for Paul, Matthew, Mark, or Luke? How about Moses, the Hebrew boys, Daniel, or Jeremiah? No! NO! NO! A thousand times "NO!" As a follower of Jesus, you need to know this. Jesus says the world will hate you, because it hated Him first. **John 15:18**, "If the world hates you, ye know that it hated me before it hated you." **Matthew 24:9** "Then shall they deliver you up to be afflicted, and shall kill you: and ye shall be hated of all nations for my name's sake." **Luke 6:22** "Blessed are ye, when men shall hate you, and when they shall separate you from their company, and shall reproach you, and cast out your name as evil, for the Son of man's sake." **1 John 3:13**, "Marvel not, my brethren, if the world hate you."

Again, doesn't the Bible say expressly in **2 Timothy 3:12** "Yea, and all that will live godly in Christ Jesus shall suffer persecution." We must answer the question of, what do we do when the world hates us for being a follower of Christ; followers who will not compromise on the Word of God. Do we give in, give up or give out? No! Do we disassociate ourselves from Christ? No! The world will see us as a liability regarding its geopolitically and geochurchlitically stances and views. Correctness will be defined by the majority. The

124

world will hold fast to its strict and narrow view as ordained by the powers of this world. It will see those who refuse to abandon their faith in the truths of the Bible as heretics or troublemakers. However, Christ sees something totally different. He sees His children as faithful and sold out to His glorious cause.

When you stand for Christ with a "come what may," or a "no matter what" attitude, you are not a liability as the world may judge you. You are the reliability of Christ. He knows and has always known the end from the beginning. He knew that you would run the good race all the way to the finish line. He knew that you could be counted on, that you would be reliable. If the world wants to label you as a liability for standing for Christ and His righteous ways, then let them. In fact, if you have the opportunity to do so, cry aloud, **I AM A LIABILITY TO THE WORLD, BUT A RELIABILITY TO CHRIST!**

When standing for Jesus is an earthly liability, you must embrace it. It is never bad in the eyes of God. Always remember the words of **Matthew 5:11,** "Blessed are ye, when men shall revile you, and persecute you, and shall say all manner of evil against you falsely, for my sake." Also, keep in mind **Matthew 16:25,** because we must stand! Even if we lose our earthly lives, we still have the wonderful and blessed promise of eternal life. **Matthew 16: 25** promises "For whosoever will save his life shall lose it: and whosoever will lose his life for my sake shall find it."

Aren't these perfect words of assurance? This race is truly a marathon and not a sprint. We must run this race for the long run. When one lives and stands for Christ, liability is in fact an "inherent part of the Christian journey." Those Christians truly connected to God appreciate those who faithfully follow Christ. As they hear the cries of the majority labeling them as liabilities increasing, as time draws closer to the day of our Lord's return, we can trust Jesus' words. Jesus remarks in **Mark 8:35** bears repeating. "For whosoever will save his life shall lose it; but whosoever shall lose his life for my sake and the gospel's, the same shall save it."

Listen, this race with Christ which I spoke of as a marathon is filled with obstacles, barriers, and hurdles. It is a race of endurance. **Mark 13:13** reads, "And ye shall be hated of all men for my name's sake: but he that shall endure unto the end, the same shall be saved."

Are you willing to stand and endure when everyone around you is submitting to the ways and whims of the evil one? When the world is blind and collectively sees those who are good as evil, and those who are evil as good, will you stand firm and endure? When standing is the most unpopular thing as it was for the three Hebrew boys in Babylon, "Will you have the **AUDACITY** to stand?" Your answer to this question must not only be the words from your lips, but it must also be reflected in your actions as they manifest themselves in the times ahead.

Time is the revealer of all things. What will time reveal about you? "Will you have the **AUDACITY** to stand for Christ?" He is our example. When they all cried out against Him, crucify Him, crucify Him, crucify Him! He never spoke a mumbling word. **Isaiah 53:7** declares, "He was oppressed, and he was afflicted, yet he opened not his mouth: he is brought as a lamb to the slaughter, and as a sheep before her shearers is dumb, so he openeth not his mouth."

Christ stood for us when the whole world hung in the balance. He did this while being abandoned by His disciples. He was being betrayed by Judas, while

Peter was preparing to deny Him. Thomas doubted Him, while James and John argued over who would sit on the left- and right-hand side of His earthly throne as they envisioned it. Through it all He stood firm. How about you? What will you do?

WILL YOU HAVE THE **AUDACITY** TO STAND FIRM AND ENDURE?

WELL, WILL YOU?

THE AUDACITY OF SURPRISED CHRISTIANS

God so often says to Christians that He would not have them to be ignorant. **Romans 1:13** states, "Now I would not have you ignorant, brethren…" **Romans 11:25** "For I would not, brethren, that ye should be ignorant of this mystery…" **1 Corinthians 10:1** "Moreover, brethren, I would not that ye should be ignorant…" **1 Corinthians 12:1** "Now concerning spiritual gifts, brethren, I would not have you ignorant…" **1 Thessalonians 4:13** "But I would not have you to be ignorant, brethren, concerning them which are asleep…" **2 Peter 3:8** "But, beloved, be not ignorant…" I am hopeful that you are getting the point.

It has been said that God does not like ugly, which is a statement not found in the Bible. In fact, the word "ugly" cannot be found in the entirety of the King James Version of the Bible from Genesis to Revelation. However, we can see and confirm scripturally that God does not like ignorance multiple times in His word. On this subject, allow me to say one additional thing. It is one thing to BE ignorant, but it is utterly another matter to STAY IGNORANT. I call these types of people, who choose to stay ignorant, willfully ignorant. God is aware of this sort of person. **2 Peter 3:5**, echoes His awareness, "For this they willingly are ignorant…"

Most so-called Christians will be caught completely off guard. This is not an arbitrary or presumptuous statement. The Bible supports this assertion. **Matthew 7:22-23** shows us an image of the so-called Christians' surprise. It says, "Many will say to me in that day, Lord, Lord, have we not prophesied in thy name? and in thy name have cast out devils? and in thy name done many wonderful works? 23 And then will I profess unto them, **I never knew you:** depart from me, ye that work iniquity."

We spoke earlier of the directions from which the enemy will make his assaults. We emphasized that it would be from the most unlikely and unsuspecting sources. This is not about from which direction the attack will come. It is much more about "from whom" the attack will emanate.

It will be from the least likely suspects. It will be those in whom you have invested your trust. Even though the Bible clearly tells us, to not place our trust in any man, not even a prince or a friend. **Psalm 146:3** testifies "Put not your trust in princes, nor in the son of man, in whom there is no help." **Micah 7:5**, gets personal by saying, "Trust ye not in a friend…"

The Bible states where the surprise attacks might come from in this manner in **Micah 7:6.** "For the son dishonoureth the father, the daughter riseth up against her mother, the daughter in law against her mother in law; **a man's enemies are the men of his own house."**

This is not just about your brothers, sisters and family members who carry your esteemed bloodline or DNA. This is something far more sinister. This refers also to your brothers and sisters in Christ. These are those we call the church, those who are a part of the household and family of faith. The following Bible texts will be revealing. They will show you the three sources of destructive darkness operating behind and in front of the scene against the church and the believers therein. These sources will spur the attacks from those **fact-lazy** people that are near and dear to us. **Matthew 7:15** warns, "Beware of **false prophets**, which come to you in sheep's clothing, but inwardly they are ravening wolves." **Matthew 10:16** cautions, "Behold, I send you forth as sheep in the midst of wolves be ye therefore wise as serpents, and harmless as doves." **Matthew 13:30,** speaking of the wheat and tares occupying the church, commands, "Let both grow together until the harvest: and in the time of harvest, I will say to the reapers, Gather ye together first the tares, and bind them in bundles to burn them: but gather the wheat into my barn."

So, we have three various entities merging to obtain one common outcome, **the destruction of the Church** of the Living God. We have identified as number one, the **False prophets, or wolves in sheep clothing,** who have already entered the church. These are powerful men and women who are ordained of hell, while glowing with the appearance of heavenly angels.

We will find these wolves exalted and elevated in leadership positions in our churches. Therefore, we must be very deep into the study of the Bible which helps us to recognize them. The Bible is the food of sheep. **Luke 4:4** reads, "And Jesus answered him, saying, It is written, That man shall not live by bread alone, but by every word of God." Did you hear that? "Every word of God."

As sheep we must grasp the importance of having an acute awareness of what our status as sheep means. We must always be fully cognizant of our surroundings and the dangerous wolves lurking therein. Because we are among the worst sort of wolves; the ravenous, rapacious, and predatory type, we must ever have our eyes on the Good Shepherd. This is the beginning of wisdom. **Always Watch, stay close to, and obey the Good Shepherd**.

We are much less likely to be surprised when our eyes are on the Good Shepherd as we walk in His will. **Mark 13:37** Says, "And what I say unto you I say unto all, **Watch**." I love the song, "Turn Your Eyes Upon Jesus." We simply must closely attend to and watch the Good Shepherd!

The second enemy (number 2), that is melding his powers with the first enemy is the devil himself. All around us there are those who are engaged in and mesmerized by Satan in his many and various forms. Those professing to speak with the dead have never truly spoken with the dead.

Ecclesiastes 9:5 exclaims, "For the living know that they shall die: but the dead know not anything, neither have they any more a reward; for the memory of them is forgotten."

You cannot speak with the dead. They are dead. That is exactly what "dead" means, DEAD. The Bible says that the dead know not anything. That means that they have no consciousness. They do not know their name, where they are from, where they lived or ANYTING. It goes on to say that they have no memory. It does not say this because they are alive and absentminded. It says this because they are dead. Finally, it says that they have no consciousness. They have no conscious thoughts or awareness. Why? Because they are dead.

This may cause you to ask, well then to whom is my psychic talking. Here is the answer. If they are not some type of scam artists, then they are speaking with demons. The Bible says in **Revelation 12:7,** "And there was war in heaven: Michael and his angels fought against the dragon; and the dragon fought and his angels." This next verse lets us know who the dragon is, **Revelation 20:2** says, "And he laid hold on the **dragon**, that old **serpent, which is the Devil, and Satan**, and bound him a thousand years."

So thus far we know that there was a war in heaven with the dragon, and that dragon is identified as the devil and Satan. Let's consider this next truth.

Revelation 12:9 tells us, "And the great dragon was cast out, that old serpent, called the Devil, and Satan, which deceiveth the whole world: **he was cast out into the earth, and his angels were cast out with him.**"

So, now we can see that after the devil lost the war in heaven he was cast to the earth. However, it did not just say that he, the devil was cast to the earth. It also says, "and his angels were cast out with him."

This is who your psychic is speaking with; they are fallen angels known as demons. We are told to stay away from them, because we can unwittingly give them access to our minds where they can actually possess us. Stay away from these sorts of people. **Leviticus 19:31** counsels us, "Regard not them that have familiar spirits, neither seek after wizards, **to be defiled by them**: I am the Lord your God." Do you hear God warning us against being possessed by these spirits? He says that we can **"be defiled by them."**

If we disobey God in this important matter, He will cut us off from His people or His true church. **Leviticus 20:6** says, "And the soul that turneth after such as have familiar spirits, and after wizards, to go a whoring after them, I will even set my face against that soul, and will **cut him off from among his people**."

To deal with familiar spirits in the early days of Israel was so egregious that those who did so were put to death. **Leviticus 20:27** is clear on this subject. "A man also or woman that hath a familiar spirit, or that is a wizard, shall **surely be put to death**: they shall stone them with stones: their blood shall be upon them."

Listen, these demons have roamed the face of the earth before sin entered the world. They are familiar with every human being upon the face of the earth. That is why it is so easy for them to give personal information on your deceased loved ones. These demons know how they acted, how they talked, what interest them most, etc.

Avoid dealing with these dark powers as if they were the plague. I remember as a young kid watching entertainers on the Ed Sullivan and the Tonight Show. These were entertainers that could imitate the voice patterns and speech of various Hollywood stars. They were so good in fact, that if you closed your eyes, you could not discern if it was the actual star or the impersonator speaking.

If a human being can do that, imagine what demons can do. Perhaps they can try to communicate directly with you if you entertain them. If you dare to embark upon their enchanted grounds, you have no idea what you are setting yourself up for **NO TRESPASSING – STAY AWAY!** You can play with the devil, but the devil does not play.

These foul spirits cannot only audibly imitate those loved ones, but can even appear as apparitions, ghosts, ghouls, spirits, and phantoms. Have nothing to do with this dark and evil world of occultism. If you have been doing this unknowingly, ask God for forgiveness and turn away from it immediately. God is still full of grace. The Bible says in **Acts 17:30,** "And the times of this ignorance God winked at; but now commandeth all men everywhere to repent."

When it comes to Satan and his demons and the evil they perpetrate, we must understand that they have been around for thousands of years. Not only this, but these demonic entities have been in heaven in the very presence of God. We can never contend with these powerful forces on our own. God knows this and has put everything in place to keep us safe and protected. In His love and mercy, He makes them powerless to communicate with us.

However, God's love will not allow Him to force or compel us to stay away from them. It is the same as it was in the Garden of Eden. The serpent could not approach Adam or Eve. They had to approach him. If they had never approached him, they would never have been seduced by his wiles, trickeries, deceit, and deceptions.

God admonishes us to stay away from Satan and to not allow him or his imps to come near us. Listen, I do not go to any movies or shows where the occult is involved. I do not listen to any music that glorifies evil or the devil who is the ultimate source of evil. There is a reason for my behavior. Watching evil as entertainment is extremely dangerous. It turns people toward it and away from God. Then the evil attaches itself to them, which sounds a lot like possessing them. The Bible says in, "**Psalm 101:3** "I will set **no wicked thing before mine eyes**, I hate the work of them that **turn aside**; it shall not **cleave to me**.

How can this happen to us, you might ask? The answer is found in **2 Corinthians 3:18**. "But we all, with open face **beholding** as in a glass the glory of the Lord, **are changed** into the same image from glory to glory, even as by the **Spirit of the Lord**. It says that as we behold or look upon the glory of the

Lord, we are changed into His image, by the Spirit of the Lord." Likewise, we must reason that if we behold or look upon evil that glorifies Satan, we will be changed into his image by his evil spirits.

Stay away from it all! Horoscopes, or as I like to say horror-scopes, Ouija-boards, tarot cards, palm readers, psychics, necromancers, wizards, witches, shows about the dead, Dracula, voodoo, the occult, Frankenstein, warlocks, enchanters, sorcerers, hypnotist, conjurers, illusionists, prestidigitators, those dealing in magic, the paranormal, levitation, diviners, spiritualists, mystics, telepathists, clairvoyants, mind readers, devil worshipers, or games that replicate any of these dark entities.

We have introduced the wolves in sheep clothing. They are the wolves in God's church represented by the false prophets and false ministers. These leaders' sole purpose is to profit from and fleece the sheep. Isn't it amazing of what the Lord asked Peter in **John 21:15-17.** "So when they had dined, Jesus saith to Simon Peter, Simon, son of Jonas, **lovest thou me** more than these? He saith unto him, Yea, Lord; thou knowest that I love thee. He saith unto him, **Feed my lambs.** 16 He saith to him again the second time, Simon, son of Jonas, **lovest thou me**? He saith unto him, Yea, Lord; thou knowest that I love thee. He saith unto him, **Feed my sheep.** 17 He saith unto him the third time, Simon, son of Jonas, **lovest thou me**? Peter was grieved because he said unto him the third time, Lovest thou me? And he said unto him, Lord, thou knowest all things; thou knowest that I love thee. Jesus saith unto him, **Feed my sheep**." Isn't it wonderful that God equates loving Him with feeding the sheep of the church? However, what occurs more times than not, is that the sheep are feeding the earthly shepherds or hirelings. I know that a laborer is worthy of his hire, but come on, the stuff that I am seeing is utterly ridiculous. I get angry because I hear a certain celebrity telling the truth. He says something along the line of seeing insincere money hogs taking advantage of their members who really love God. Okay, enough of that, but I had to say what I feel was placed on my heart by the Spirit of God. So back to our points being made.

We also introduced, at least in part, Satan, and his fallen demons, who are at the forefront of attacking the church via spiritualism. This attack is orchestrated to deceive the church by telling them and the world that the dead are not really dead. The **AUDACITY** of the arch enemy of God in telling this lie is nothing new. We find him espousing a terribly similar lie through the serpent in the Garden of Eden. We see this unfold in **Genesis 3:4.** "And the serpent said unto the woman, Ye shall not surely die." What a lie! King Solomon had it right when he said, there is nothing new under the sun.

Let's look deeper into the enemy's diabolical scheme to deceive and defeat the church. **Revelation 16:13** reads, "And I saw three unclean spirits like frogs come out of the mouth of the **dragon**, and out of the mouth of the **beast**, and out of the mouth of the **false prophet**. Notice that we have already spoken about the **dragon** and the **false prophet**. However, there is a third power that merges with these two to further carry out their surprise attacks on the church of the Living God. It is the beast power. Those who are unaware of this deadly and lethal set of triplets, or this triad of evil enemies against the church, will not only be surprised, but overwhelmed by the identity of their adversaries.

So, who is this beast power? We find our answer in the book of Daniel. **Daniel 7:17** identifies these beasts by saying, "These great beasts, which are four, are **four kings,** which shall arise out of the earth. So, these beasts are kings." However, we all know that kings rule kingdoms. Daniel brings further clarity to this issue in **Daniel 7:23.** "Thus he said, The fourth beast shall be the **fourth kingdom** upon earth, which shall be diverse from **all kingdoms**, and shall devour the whole earth, and shall tread it down, and break it in pieces."

In a nutshell, the beast powers are modern day earthly rulers. These rulers are Presidents, Prime Ministers, Kings, Queens, Emperors, Chancellors, Amirs. Shahs, etc. who are the heads of vast earthly domains, states, countries, empires, and kingdoms. When these states, **nations**, or political entities join with these churches or **false prophets** and the **dark spiritual powers** of this world, there will be laws and decrees written and enacted to revile and attack the church of the Living God. This assault will be enforced in ways that are now unfathomable to us. These cataclysmic events are unfolding before blind eyes that are physically capable of vision, but they are blind because they are spiritually shut.

The surprise will be swift and sudden. It will come from those who do not love God and do not love truth. This may sound bizarre, but you cannot love God and hate truth. God is love, and God is Truth. In **John 14:6** "Jesus saith unto him, I am the way, the truth, and the life: no man cometh unto the Father, but by me." Jesus is the Truth. If you do not love truth, then the three aforementioned evil entities will destroy you through their prodigious, exceptional, and entrancing deceptions.

2 Thessalonians 2:10-12 makes this noticeably clear. "And with all deceivableness of unrighteousness in them that perish; because they **received not the love of the truth**, that they might be **saved**. 11 And for this cause God shall send them strong delusion, that they should **believe a lie**: 12 That they all might be damned who believed not the truth, but had pleasure in unrighteousness."

The Bible makes it clear that people will be lost because they do not have a LOVE for the truth.

155

They listen to preachers and teachers who are not grounded in God's word. Be aware that I am saying this while acknowledging that many pastors are truly in love with God and do an excellent job of shepherding the flock.

I am referring here to the hirelings. These poor sheep will believe anything coming out of these false prophets' mouths. Yet, when confronted with the very word of God itself, they will not believe a plain "Thus saith the Lord." Many will not believe the Bible because they remain comfortable as **lazy-fact** people who do not search and read the scriptures daily for themselves.

Notice what the Bible has to say about the NOBLE men of Berea as it compares them to those in Thessalonica. **Acts 17:11** says, "These were more noble than those in Thessalonica, in that they **received the word with all readiness of mind, and searched the scriptures daily**, whether those things were so." The Bereans, instead of running from the truths of God, received that truth with a ready and willing spirit. Still, they did not stop there. They studied and searched the scripture daily to **confirm** that what had been spoken to them could be affirmed in the Word of God.

You cannot allow anyone to spoon-feed you their version of biblical truths. These are life and death matters being weighed in the balances of eternity. You should not and must not do that! You must be able to give an account of what you believe from the scriptures that you have read for yourself. It is a blessing from God, that now for those who cannot read, the Bible is on various digital formats that can be listened to repeatedly.

Allow me to go back to a point made earlier, but not explored. **Matthew 13:29-30** "But he said, Nay; lest while ye gather up the tares, ye root up also the wheat with them. 30 **Let both grow together** until the harvest: and in the time of harvest I will say to the reapers, Gather ye together first the tares, and bind them in bundles to burn them: but gather the wheat into my barn."

Please note that the wheat represents the children of God, but the tares represent the children of the devil. Notice at the beginning of verse thirty, it says let both the wheat and tares grow together. This gives us a particularly good picture of God's church. There will be both wolves and sheep in the church. There will also be wheat and tares in the church. To be candid, Jesus had wolves and tares in His own church while here on earth. Judas was there, in the midst of the apostles, comprising the church that Jesus shepherded. Judas was right there until the kiss of betrayal and disloyalty that he gave to Christ in the Garden of Gethsemane.

This tells me not to look for a perfect church on earth before the second return of Christ our Savior and Lord. There will be liars, fornicators, adulterers, thieves, blasphemers, hypocrites, gossipers, you name it. They could be operating anywhere in the house of God, from the back of the church to the pulpit and choir loft.

You cannot control other people. You may have some influence, but never control. It is your responsibility to live the best Christian life that you can by God's sweet grace and tender mercies. Do not try to prematurely call out wolves and tares. That is God's job. Treat them better than they treat you.

Oh, dear believers, there **is** a place and time for everything under the sun. God has reserved the exposure of these wolves and tares toward the end of time. We know this because he said that exposure would occur during the "harvest." We only harvest that which is ripe or fully grown. God's way is not only the best way, but also the only way that nets the results that heaven desires.

Right now, wheat and tares are occupying the same pulpits, pews, and offices in our churches. We must not focus our energies so much on ridding the church of these perpetrators, and pretenders. I repeat, the Word of God says that they will grow together until the harvest (the return of Jesus). However, I do not want you to get the idea that we are powerless here. We can and must do our part. Our part is for to simply, **"BE LIGHT."** By the grace and help of God, we must commit ourselves to be the very best, loving, compassionate, and wise Christians possible.

John 8:12 tells us, "Then spake Jesus again unto them, saying, I am the **light of the world**: he that followeth me shall not walk in darkness, but shall **have the light** of life." When wayward souls enter the church, be there to let them see what God looks like through you. Do not abandon your churches because of the foul spirits inhabiting some members and/or leaders. Just think, if all true believers abandoned the church, who will be left to greet those "wondering and wandering" sheep who are hungering and thirsting after righteousness?

Did Jesus not show us that many of the members of His initial and formational church were flawed and sinful. Look at what the disciples, all of them, did on the night that Jesus allowed Himself to be taken prisoner. **Matthew 26:55-56** says, "In that same hour said Jesus to the multitudes, Are ye come out as against a thief with swords and staves for to take me? I sat daily with you teaching in the temple, and ye laid no hold on me. 56 But all this was done, that the scriptures of the prophets might be fulfilled. Then **ALL the disciples forsook him and fled**." Mark puts it a bit more succinctly, **Mark 14:50** "And they **all forsook him, and fled**." Does that sound like a perfect church? This event occurred after Jesus had been with them teaching, preaching, and working miracles for about three and a half years. Peter would deny Him. Judas would betray Him. James and John would covet the seats on the left and right-hand side of what they perceived would be

His earthly throne. Thomas would doubt Him. These flawed and imperfect mortals are those chosen by Christ to comprise and constitute the church of the Living God.

Dear fellow believers do not look for a perfect church on this earth until after Jesus has made all things new. Listen to **2 Corinthians 5:17** "Therefore if any man be in Christ, he is a new creature: old things are passed away; behold, all things are become new."

This does not mean that we should not strive for perfection in Christ. **Philippians 4:13** tell us, "I can do all things through Christ which strengtheneth me." However, we must recognize that nothing can be accomplished without Christ. In fact, we are powerless do anything without Christ. We cannot take our next breath in or breathe it out without Jesus.

In **John 15:5** Jesus declares, "I am the vine, ye are the branches: He that abideth in me, and I in him, the same bringeth forth much fruit: for **without me ye can do nothing**. "Nothing means just that, nothing**! John 9:33** adds, "If this man were not of God, **he could do nothing."** So, our movement toward perfection begins with and ends with God.

Wolves on the other hand do not desire to strive for the kingdom of God. They do not desire the perfection and blessed cleansing afforded believers by His precious and sacred shed-blood. Wolves are satisfied being wolves. They quickly become acclimated to sheep clothing. This occurs easily because their constant reinforcement is having continual access to the sheep. Understand, that when wolves look at sheep, all they can see are meals consisting of tender and juicy lamb-chops.

Why should we get upset with wolves for being who they are, wolves? We cannot blame wolves for being their distinctive wolfish selves. We cannot cry foul on their part for following their innate savage and unconstrained tendencies. Wolves do what wolves do! So, wolves acting as wolves is not our concern. What is our concern, is the fact that the sheep are failing to recognize wolves for who and what they are.

Pay close attention to these next few statements. It is imperative, as mentioned earlier, that our eyes are opened. Yet, open eyes are useless if they are blind. This blindness that presently exists will continue to exist as long as sheep are without a rich knowledge of the Word of God.

It is the Word of God that X-rays, examines, and dissect every flawed character-trait of wolves. It exposes them for the ravenous beasts that they are. Often, wolves hide behind and are protected by their high offices or their status and rank in the church. Ever more often, we are afraid to open our mouths because of how the wolves and the other sheep might respond to our utterances. Our silence emboldens and compels them to be more brazen, daring, and brash. This is not asking anyone to call anyone out as tares or wolves. What this is saying is simply this. We must speak up against any evil that attempts to injure the church.

We can respond against the actions of a person without attacking the person. We are protective of the church, because it is where God has planted us to be His arbiters of the gospel and alert and loving watchmen. As watchmen, when we see the enemy raising his sword to injure the church, we are mandated, and must sound the alarm. **Ezekiel 33:6** expresses, "But if the watchman see the sword come, and blow not the trumpet, and the people be not warned; if the sword come, and take any person from among them, he is taken away in his iniquity; but his blood will I require at the watchman's hand."

When we see children of God being injured and abused by wolves and tares, we must not be idle and voiceless at such a time. In love, blow the trumpet's warning sound and let the Word of God reconcile the situation in spirit and truth.

Knowing that these dangerous and predatory wolves are among us should cause us to be more vigilant. As watchmen, we must be extremely attentive and alert. We must especially investigate ourselves. However, when we begin this undertaking, it is of vital importance that we recognize that the only mirror to be used is the Bible, the Word of the Living God.

Dr. J. Calvin Alberty

If you are not, by the sanctifying and consecrating power of God's goodness and grace, making an earnest effort to live up to His holy standards, then do not try to change the mirror. Make every effort to invite the Holy Spirit to take control of the one holding the mirror in their hand. The Amazing and life altering Holy Spirit can still turn old dirty filthy wolves into beautiful born-again sheep, who have been washed in the blood of Jesus. Hallelujah!

This self-investigation is enormously necessary. This is the case because many of us have unknowingly and unwittingly been under the tutelage and guidance of some of these very sly and stealthy wolves.

Let's go deeper here. No matter how vigilant we are as sheep, we need the Good Shepherd, not the hireling, to look after us. Among our ranks are those who will not sound the trumpet of warning, because they are blind, ignorant, or fast asleep. The Word of God says in **Isaiah 56:10** "His watchmen are blind: they are all ignorant, they are all dumb dogs, they cannot bark; sleeping, lying down, loving to slumber."

In the time in which we live, we are not allowed the luxury of being ignorant to what is happening around us. It is an extremely dangerous time to be sleeping when we should be wide awake and watchful. It is written in **Romans 13:11** "And that, knowing the time, that now it is **high time to**

awake out of sleep: for now, is our salvation nearer than when we believed."

With all that we have considered within the context of these pages, we must expressly and explicitly acknowledge that sheep are helpless without a very good shepherd, as I stated earlier. This is where the need for wisdom is catapulted to the forefront. In nature, SHEEP ARE NOT VERY SUCCESSFUL IN FIGHTING AGAINST WOLVES! ONLY THE SHEPHERD CAN DO THAT. However, the sheep can RUN TO THE SHEPHERD.

Sheep are not to be watchful or alert for the purpose of fighting wolves. They are to be alert to always knowing the location of the Good Shepherd. They want to keep close to him and keep their running distance as short as possible between them and the shepherd. The entire 23rd Psalm proclaims and declares the keeping power of the shepherd, and the peace that the sheep enjoy in the Good Shepherd's presence.

Take your time on the next page and read deeply and slowly. Please meditate on what each verse means to you.

Dr. J. Calvin Alberty

THE 23RD PSALM

1 The Lord is my shepherd; I shall not want.

*2 He maketh me to lie down in green pastures: he
leadeth me beside the still waters.*

*3 He restoreth my soul: he leadeth me in the paths of
righteousness for his name's sake.*

*4 Yea, though I walk through the valley of the shadow
of death, I will fear no evil: for thou art with me; thy
rod and thy staff they comfort me.*

*5 Thou preparest a table before me in the presence of
mine enemies: thou anointest my head with oil; my
cup runneth over.*

*6 Surely goodness and mercy shall follow me all the
days of my life: and I will dwell in the house of the
Lord forever.*

It is so important that the sheep recognize the shepherd's voice. While thumbing through the channels on my television, I briefly stumbled upon and began watching a show on hunters. Some hunted ducks, others hunted wild turkeys, and others hunted deer. After only a brief time, I noticed this one thing that they all had in common. Each of the hunters had some type of device that created sounds that brought their prey into closer proximity to their weapons. Had the prey only recognized that the sounds or voices beckoning them near were not genuine or authentic, they would have remained at a safe distance.

Even more importantly, had they remained close to the shepherd they would have been safe.

The shepherd would have warned them that the sounds were counterfeit. He also would have taught them to run away from such sounds and run toward the Good Shepherd. This tells us that it is especially important that we, as Christians, know the difference between the voice of the Good Shepherd as opposed to the voice of the enemy of souls. Knowing that we are among wolves and tares should magnify this point even more. **1 John 4:1** highlights this point when it says, "Beloved, believe not every spirit, but try the spirits whether they are of God: because many false prophets are gone out into the world."

Again, the wheat represents the truth loving Christians of Christ, while the tares represent those who follow another more sinister and darker voice.

John 10:4 declares that we will know our Shepherd and He will know His Sheep. It says, "And when he putteth forth his own sheep, he goeth before them, and the sheep follow him: for they know his voice."

This is a recurring theme in the Bible. In heaven the angel Lucifer became a devil and had to be thrown out. He was blessed to be right there, in the direct presence of God, yet Lucifer's jealousy, evil, hate, and deceitfulness began shaping the character of this angel of light. He had been created in perfection. Lucifer's failure was listening to his own narcissistic voice instead of the voice of God.

In the Garden of Eden, Adam and Eve, enjoyed the most perfect paradise until they chose to listen to and believe the voice of a lying serpent over the words of a tender and loving God. They believed a lie instead of the truth.

Another example of this theme is when one brother, Cain, murders his younger brother Abel. He would do so simply because Abel was obedient to the voice or command of God. Instead of doing the right thing as God had commanded him, Cain chose instead to ignore His creator's voice and murder his brother for following those same dictates of his loving Creator.

Jacob and Esau continue this theme. These two twins contended with one another while still in their mother's womb. They both listened to voices that did not emanate from God. Jacob lied to his father and Esau did not respect his birthright. They lived at odds with one another until Jacob fled for his life. Their descendants to this very day, continue their debates, disputations, and contentions.

In the very ranks of Christ's disciples, Judas stood in opposition to Christ's way of establishing His church and kingdom. Instead of listening to Christ and catching a glimpse of His vision, Judas instead listened to the religious leaders who were prompted by the workings of Satan.

Christ kingdom was to be eternal, but Judas attempted to force Christ's hand and compel Him to establish an impermanent earthly kingdom in which he, Judas could for a brief period exalt himself. Instead of accepting and embracing the truths spoken by the Son of God, Judas betrayed Jesus in pursuit of his own agenda for thirty pieces of filthy silver.

Religious sects, in this world, have fought many wars and carried on murderous crusades and campaigns in the name of Jesus or their gods. They had the **AUDACITY** to term these clashes as "Holy Wars." It is everything but holy when fiendish men attempt to impose their will on other men. This is exactly what happened. Evil men sought to compel free moral beings, who were created by God, to worship God in a manner that went contrary their own conscience.

They tried to control not merely who these free moral agents worshipped, but even the manner of how they worshipped. Instead of allowing mankind, who God gifted with the power of choice, to worship according to his conscience, they fought to oppress him. They efforted to compel them to subjugate their God given will and surrender it to their oppressors. They used every foul and murderous form of torture and humiliation that entered their demented and sick minds.

The overarching message here is, do not be surprised when the greatest and most damaging injury to your Christian experience turns out to be from within your own household of faith, provoked by the adversary of God. This idea is not new at all. After all, didn't Satan provoke the church in Paul's day to stone the faithful Stephen, the first recorded Christian Martyr, to death?

Wasn't it the church that was provoked by Satan to seek out Roman leaders to crucify Jesus?

The unpreparedness of the church for this incomprehensible reality will cause the household of faith to be one group of shocked, stunned, and surprised brothers and sisters. Can you imagine those of like faith, whom we have worshipped with for many years, turning on one another? Can you imagine hearing words of betrayal flowing freely from the mouths of those that you once deeply trusted. This is exactly what happened in the past, and these inexplicable disgusting and repulsive acts will repeat themselves according to the unfaltering Word of God. **Matthew 10:36** testifies, "And a man's foes shall be they of his own household." **Matthew 24:10** strengthens this text of scripture with these words, "And then shall many be offended, and shall betray one another, and shall hate one another." There is more. **Mark 13:12** adds, "Now the brother shall betray the brother to death, and the father the son; and children shall rise up against their parents and shall cause them to be put to death."

> **As the signs unfold before your very eyes,**
>
> **Please be aware, but never surprised.**

You must not be surprised when those spiritual leaders that you love and so very much respect turn against you. You must not be caught off guard when they revile you and the entire world says amen. You will study to prepare yourself for what is ahead. Will you study, according to **2 Timothy 2:15,**

to show yourself approved unto God? "Study to shew

thyself approved unto God, a workman that needeth

not to be ashamed, rightly dividing the word of truth."

Will you study and live what is learned with all your

heart?

Will you study, study, study?

WELL, WILL YOU?

THE AUDACITY OF BEING PECULIAR

That which is peculiar, odd, or different tends to draw attention to itself. God tells us in **1 Peter 2:9,** "But ye are a chosen generation, a royal priesthood, an holy nation, a **peculiar** people; that ye should shew forth the praises of him who hath called you out of darkness into his marvelous light;" **Titus 2:14** amplifies the peculiarity of you and I as Christians with these words. "Who gave himself for us, that he might redeem us from all iniquity, and purify unto himself a **peculiar people**, zealous of good works." **Deuteronomy 26:18** "And the Lord hath avouched thee this day to be his **peculiar people**, as he hath promised thee, and that thou shouldest **keep all his commandments**;" These few texts should make it obvious that we are to be different from the world. **John 17:14** "I have given them thy word; and the world hath hated them, because they are **not of the world**, even as I am not of the world." Our conversations are different from the conversations of the world. **Philippians 3:20** "For our conversation is in heaven; from whence also we look for the Saviour, the Lord Jesus Christ:"

The problem with being different, is that many of us are uncomfortable with the difference that Christ not only desires of us but requires of us. As the world grows darker, because of God's Spirit being withdrawn, your light will appear brighter. The unique light of God pouring through you will make you stand out in the darkness. It is a darkness that is becoming denser and more pronounced. You must be prepared to stand alone with and for the Lord! There will be no help from the world during these times, but the entirety of God, through the Holy Spirit and the holy angels will be right by your side. So, always remember the words of Christ in **Matthew 28:20.** "…**LO, I AM WITH YOU ALWAYS**, even unto the end of the world. Amen." **Hebrews 13:5** amplifies this text with these words, "Let your conversation be without covetousness; and be content with such things as ye have: for **he hath said, I will never leave thee, nor forsake thee**. 6 So that we may boldly say, **The Lord is my helper, and <u>I will not fear what man shall do unto me</u>.**

Dr. J. Calvin Alberty

Are you prepared to not only stand up, but to also to stand out as a lone voice, a lone believer, or a lone disciple of Christ? Are you willing to stand up and out proclaiming the gospel of Jesus Christ? If we do just a little research, we will see that people in the Bible and outside of the Bible have been willing to sacrifice all for that which they passionately believed in and revered as sacred.

We find in these people, who dared to have the **AUDACITY** to be peculiar, no ordinary strength. By the power of the Holy Spirit, they are willing to embrace being labeled a liability by the world. With God residing in their hearts, they will be strong-minded, unwavering Christians striving for the excellence of His glory. As we have just cited from the book of Hebrews, they will boldly profess, "I will not fear what man shall do unto me."

If we look at these individual more closely, we will discover in every case that EXCELLENCE always partners with LIABILITY for God. Consider these few champions of their time. Think of their courage, their great feats, and persistent nature, in the cause of God. Think of how their faith and determination led them to their incredible discoveries and unparalleled successes.

1. **The Wright Brothers** were told innumerous times that flight was impossible. They were so **peculiar** until even their father, who was a minister, was quoted as saying, "Men will never fly, because flying is reserved for angels." In 1908 Orville Wright took a

young Lieutenant from the army on a flight. The plane crashed and killed the young officer. I am sure that scoffers were plenteous in naming him a liability.

The Wright brothers, having been given this label of liability, after the young lieutenant's death, must have been highly discouraged, but they still had the **AUDACITY** to persist in their effort to conquer the air; and because they did, today we have supersonic jets and rockets. We have landed on the moon and ascended to the outer realm of our solar system.

2. Abraham Lincoln

It required a decisive and special man to try to bring a fractured country together. This was especially the case when the subject matter was such an explosive issue like slavery. Yet, the **peculiar** Abraham Lincoln stood firm. A people of beauty were freed. Lincoln greatly increased his liability for personal harm as he stood on the righteous side of justice and morality. The **AUDACITY** of this one courageous man would cost him his earthly life, but his greater good could not be silenced with an assassin's bullet. His life would live out its **purpose** with **passion** that would **persist** in changing the course of history forever.

3. George Washington

The **AUDACITY** of George Washington to fight for independence in a war that was thought to be unwinnable and yet succeed is remarkable.

4. <u>Martin Luther King Jr.</u>

The **AUDACITY** of Martin Luther King Jr. to make his **peculiar** dream a reality at the peril of his own life is inconceivable. To hear him define his **purpose** by crying out **"I just want to do God's will,"** gives insight into his great moral compass. To see his family placed in peril was unnerving and frightening. Yet, to see him **passionately** emerge from the ashes of terrorists' bombs was awe inspiring. His **persistency** in championing the cause of freedom, despite the racist threats on his life, was incredible. His purpose, passion, and persistence depict his profound level of conviction to a movement that a sniper's bullet could not kill.

5. The **AUDACITY** of the **peculiar** Nelson Mandela.
He would say "no" to apartheid and inequality. He did
so not merely by his words, but by his deeds. His
passion was freedom and equality for all. His
purpose was to sacrifice everything necessary, to
include his life, for the accomplishment of his
purpose. He **persisted** through 27 years of
incarceration in a South African prison. His
unrelenting and unwavering spirit of justice and
equality for all, united the people of South Africa to
elect him as the first Black president of their country.

6. Mahatma Gandhi

The **AUDACITY** of the **peculiar** Indian activist to
stand up to British colonial rule. He inspired Dr. King

and so many others by choosing an approach of nonviolence to win independence for his people.

7. <u>Countless others</u>

The **<u>AUDACITY</u>** of countless other **peculiar** Christian martyrs to lay down their lives to exalt the cause of Christ and religious freedom is an affirmation of their love for God.

How about us dear believer in Christ? Do we have that fiery **<u>AUDACITY</u>** to be **peculiar**? You and I have been privileged by God to perhaps be the very last generation upon the earth. We could be that generation that witnesses the return of Christ. This should be great news for all who are preparing for His return. However, we should also have an intimate knowledge of the biblical description of what that return will look like, and the challenges that lie ahead for us in these last days of earth's history as we now know it.

The world will be in turmoil. History will repeat itself. The church will again be persecuted. Many so-called Christians will turn away from God and attempt to impose their will on those who are loyal to the Savior. They will do everything within their power to compel God's people to worship God in a manner that is contrary to scriptural dictates. These times will be traumatic and trying. They will test the very limits of our core commitment to God.

Please do not think that it was happenstance that you were born at such a time as this. Those peculiar champions I listed from the past worked untiringly in paving roads to a better world. Some operated under the authority and power of Christ. They worked toward their purposes until they could work no more. God had them on His mind before they were ever called into existence. He knew them intimately before they took their first breath.

It is now our time to come to the forefront in the Army of Christ. We, as the called of God, were born for this moment. God has called us into existence for this very unique and tumultuous time. He declares in **Jeremiah 29:11** "For I know the thoughts that I think toward you, saith the Lord, thoughts of peace, and not of evil, to give you an expected end." Do you comprehend the gravity of this verse of scripture? God had you on His mind before you were ever created. His thoughts and plans for you are good and not evil.

Cyrus is one such person who was in God's plans before he was conceived in his mother's womb. We read in **Isaiah 45:1**, "Thus saith the Lord to his anointed, to Cyrus, whose right hand I have holden, to subdue nations before him; and I will loose the loins of kings, to open before him the two leaved gates; and the gates shall not be shut."

We know that this statement about Cyrus, who would become king of the Medo-Persian empire, was written in scripture about one hundred years before he was born. It was in direct fulfillment of the words of the Bible. Cyrus entered Babylon through the two leaved gates and conquered the city that was thought by all to be unconquerable.

Just as God had prophesied through Isaiah in the 45th chapter of the book bearing Isaiah's name, Cyrus entered the scene right on time with prophecy. The Book of Isaiah was written between 701-681 BC. Cyrus was born somewhere between 580 and 600 BC. This means that this prophecy could have been given as much as 121 years before Cyrus was born. Isn't that incredible?

Before closing this chapter, it is important to add the perspective of Queen Esther and her relative Mordecai. This perspective is found in the fourth chapter of the book of Esther, beginning with verse 14. Evil Haman has tricked the King into declaring a death decree upon the people of God, the Jews. Mordecai is the relative that raised Esther. He believes that as queen, Esther will have enough influence to change the mind of the king and alter the death decree. Somehow, Mordecai gets a message of warning into the palace to Queen Esther.

We find his message in **Esther 4th chapter beginning with verse fourteen**. "For if thou altogether holdest thy peace at this time, then shall there enlargement and deliverance arise to the Jews from another place; but thou and thy father's house shall be destroyed: and who knoweth whether thou art come to the kingdom **for such a time as this**?" Please allow me to restate what Mordecai was saying. "Listen Esther, if you do not speak out against this murderous plot against our people, which has been perpetrated by Haman through his manipulation of the King, do not think that you will escape the forthcoming doom. If you remain silent, God will deliver us through another source, but it will not be a good thing for you and your family. All of you will be destroyed. Esther, have you ever considered that the only reason that God allowed you to become queen was for such an occasion and **such a time as this?"**

Now let's see how **Esther** responds to Mordecai, beginning with **verse fifteen of the fourth** chapter of **Esther**. "Then Esther bade them return Mordecai this answer, 16 Go, gather together all the Jews that are present in Shushan, and fast ye for me, and neither eat nor drink three days, night or day: I also and my maidens will fast likewise; and so will I go in unto the king, which is not according to the law: and **IF I PERISH, I PERISH.**"

Esther's response was one of complete dependence on God. Let every Jew in Shushan declare a three day-and-night period of fasting, and I will go in unto the king. I will go in even though I have not been summoned. To do so, Esther knew, was to risk her life. For if the king did not extend his scepter (staff) to approve her entrance into his presence, then she would be put to death.

Esther knew that she was risking it all for her people. So, she concludes with this definitive statement of commitment, "If I perish, I perish."

Dr. J. Calvin Alberty

You and I very well might perish in these
earthly bodies as we stand for Christ. As mentioned
earlier, "All that live godly in Christ Jesus shall suffer
persecution." What is the answer to this dilemma of
suffering persecution? The answer is simple, but not
so easy. You suffer the persecution for the love of
Christ. It is only those who are "**peculiar**" by their
faithfulness of adhering to God's standards that will
be persecuted for their beliefs. They will be faced
with the decision to renounce Jesus and live or
profess Jesus and die.

Truly, renouncing Jesus is never an option for
a true Christian. The motto of every Christian should
be death before failure or renunciation. Abandoning
their faith in Christ was never an option in the past,

and it is never an option for Christians now or in the future. The greatest part of our **peculiar**ity is that we never stop living for Christ." Never-never! Not Ever!

Are you peculiar for Christ?

Will you live for Him no matter what?

WELL, WILL YOU?

THE AUDACITY OF TRYING TO RUN A SPRINT!

The race is not given to the swift, but to those that endure until the end. Our race is one of endurance, not speed or quickness. We must cast aside the weights of the world and run this race with a renewed **persistency**, **purpose**, and **passion.** We must possess the drive and determination to see it through to the very end. Everything that we do should be with intentionality. This is not a race in which we can be carelessly involved. The issues are eternal in nature. The results are short-term vs. infinity, salvation vs. being loss, eternal life vs. a permanent death, and hope versus despair.

We are to run this race with every talent and gift that God has given to us. We must be willing to forsake all on behalf of Christ. The message given to Queen Esther during her time in history is now our message. That message asks each of us, "Who's to say that we were not born, at this moment in history, for such a time as this?" You and I, we are not here by accident. God knew us before we were ever conceived. He says in **Jeremiah 1:5** "Before I formed thee in the belly, I knew thee; and before thou camest forth out of the womb I sanctified thee, and I ordained thee a prophet unto the nations." Just like Jeremiah the Prophet and King Cyrus the Great, you and I were called into existence by our All-knowing, omnipotent God.

Remember, God does everything with a purpose. Before our birth, like Jeremiah and Cyrus, we were on God's mind. He prepackaged each of us with specific gifts and talents. They are ours so that we might not only be peculiar in our love for Him and humanity, but that we might have the strength and courage to endure every obstacle that life throws in our pathways. God really does know His plans for each of us and His plans really are good plans. The talents and gifts that He has given to us, He takes very seriously.

Keep in mind the biblical account of how God gave certain men talents, and the one man who wasted his talent was cast into outer darkness with dire and dreadful consequences. For such a time as this, God has created you! You came here purpose-filled with God's holy design etched into your own peculiar heart and DNA. Everything that God has placed in you has been placed there for your success in running this Christian race.

The length of this race is the same distance for every man. It is the distance of a lifetime. The prize is no different for the one who finishes first than it is for the one who finishes last. It is a crown of eternal life with God. The ultimate goal is for each of us who began running this race, to FINISH it.

You must run in the cold, the rain and snow. You must run in the sweltering heat and the mighty gales. You must run when you are sick, forsaken and alone. You must run when it is unpopular or politically incorrect. You must run when you are discouraged and disgusted. You must run when your path is filled with difficulties and complications. You must run, you must run, you must run this race as if you are running for your life! BECAUSE YOU ARE!

You must use only one standard as you run this race. That standard is our Lord Christ Jesus and no other. Do not worry about what anyone else is doing, just run. Do not be concerned about the things of tomorrow or the cares or concerns that tomorrow might bring, just run. When it appears that the whole world is against you, just run. This is the marathon of all marathons, just run! This race is to the GLORY OF **THE LIVING GOD**. Run, run, run! It is not only for now, but eternity. The goal is obtainable! Run! The goal is just ahead and in sight! Run! Oh, believers of one true God, the goal for which we run with diligence is JESUS! Run, run, run!

The devil will throw everything at you. Friends will abandon you. Husbands and wives will forsake their spouses. Friends and colleagues will betray you. When all is falling apart, the Bible says in **Luke 21:28** "And when these things begin to come to pass, then look up, and lift up your heads; for your redemption draweth nigh."

Run Christian Run! The day is far-spent, and our eternal home is nearer than ever. Run Christian Run! You are not alone in your struggles. You must have the **AUDACITY** to run the greatest of all marathons. Leave the sprints to those who focus is only in the moment. Tune your ears to the voice of the Savior. Hear Him calling out "RUN! RUN! RUN! ENDURE UNTIL YOU'RE TIRED, THEN ENDURE UNTIL THE END!"

In **1 Corinthians 2:9** God says, "Eye hath not seen, nor ear heard, neither have entered into the heart of man, the things which God hath prepared for them that love him."

Run Children Run!

Will you run?

Run Children Run!

Will you run?

Run Children Run!

Will you run?

WELL, WILL YOU?

<u>THE AUDACITY TO ENDURE THE DARKNESS</u>

One of the purer lessons of life is that it is not always sunshine. However, for some, darkness has become pervasive and inescapable. All their giddy-up appears to have gotten-up and gone. They live or exist in the fringes of darkness and shadows. Their joy has become fleeting and ephemeral. They are holding on by a tenuous, momentary, and ever fraying thread of hope. They feel that the proverbial "final straw" is about to fall, and the camel is about to be afflicted with a broken back.

The camel, witnessing what is about to happen, is groaning in the darkness. He looks around for help from a friend and sees only poor

Humpty Dumpty pathetically trying to piece his broken life back together.

In this life, things can and will go bad, quick, fast, and in a scurry-hurry. There are no timeouts. Life waits on no one. Everything continues day in and day out. Life waits on no one. There is a continuous bombardment by the enemy of souls as he persistently urges you to give up, give in, and give out. Life waits on no one. "Quit the race!" the devil urges. "It isn't worth it!" He hollers. "It's not for you!" He bellows and shouts. "You are alone, no one cares. You are too far behind and can never catch up because Life waits on no one, especially you!" He laughs. But he is scared beyond belief that you will pause and notice that Jesus, the Good Shepherd is very near. He is filled with love and all the help that you require.

You know, there is this amazing thing about God. He always loves us, and He never forsakes or abandons us. He says in **Matthew 28:20** "… lo, I am with you always, even unto the end of the world. We find in **Hebrews 13:5** … "for he hath said, I will never leave thee, nor forsake thee." **Deuteronomy 31:6** reads, "Be strong and of a good courage, fear not, nor be afraid of them: for the Lord thy God, he it is that doth go with thee; he will not fail thee, nor forsake thee." **Joshua 1:5** confirm this, "There shall not any man be able to stand before thee all the days of thy life: as I was with Moses, so I will be with thee: **I will not fail thee, nor forsake thee.**"

Four verses later we find in **Joshua 1:9** these encouraging words, "Have not I commanded thee? Be strong and of a good courage; be not afraid, neither be thou dismayed: for the Lord thy God is with thee **whithersoever thou goest**." **Isaiah 41:10** declares, "Fear thou not; for I am with thee: be not dismayed; for I am thy God: I will strengthen thee; yea, I will help thee; yea, I will uphold thee with the right hand of my righteousness."

Listen, the devil is doing everything in his power to destroy the image of God in us and in this world. He attempts to dampen our hope; challenge our faith by obscuring our vision of a concerned, loving, and caring God. He whispers that God does not care. He murmurs that God cannot be trusted.

Then comes the declaration of what he has been after all along, your life. "Life isn't worth living." He suggests. "You'll be better off dead." He stresses. "God does not care, nor does anyone else. Why suffer like this when you can have perfect peace, or when you can go to a place where no one can hurt you again, not ever."

What a set of evil, nefarious, despicable, and reprehensible lies the devil is proclaiming. There is no peace in any death without Christ. Such a death is so offensive to God, that He gave His Only Begotten Son to not allow death to be a permanent state or condition for humanity. Everything about God is good. What the devil does best is blame God for what the devil himself has done and is doing.

He creates circumstances of hardship and despair, and then declares, "God did it!" He obscures our vision of a loving and caring God, and shouts, "Where is God when you need Him?" My dear brothers and sisters, God is right there. He is holding you in the loving hollows of His compassionate hands. Even though you may not have an awareness of His loving presence, He is there.

Did not His own Son Jesus feel a similar, but much more intense pain on the cross? **Matthew 27:46** reveals, "And about the ninth hour Jesus cried with a loud voice, saying, Eli, Eli, lama sabachthani? that is to say, My God, my God, why hast thou forsaken me?"

Do you understand what happened? Do you see the humanity of Jesus experiencing the very same pains, agonies, and temptations that we as human beings experience? The Son of God felt forsaken on a level a thousand times greater than ours. The sins of the world, from Adam and Eve's downfall, all the way to Christ's second return, was oppressing and tormenting Him at that moment. Sin separates our vision and view of the Father. Listen, if Jesus, the Son of the living God, went through this, then what about us? Are we better than Jesus?

John 15:20 says, "Remember the word that I said unto you, The servant is not greater than his lord. If they have persecuted me, they will also persecute you…" In fact, **Romans 8:36** tells us, "As it is written, For thy sake we are killed all the day long; we are accounted as sheep for the slaughter."

Wow! What a statement. However, God does not leave us there. He does not leave us hopeless. In **John 14**th chapter, He tells us things like, "1 Let not your heart be troubled: ye believe in God, believe also in me. 2 In my Father's house are many mansions: if it were not so, I would have told you. I go to prepare a place for you. 3 And if I go and prepare a place for you, I will come again, and receive you unto myself; that where I am, there ye may be also." **In Isaiah 65:17** God gives us even more hope. He says, "For, behold, I create new heavens and a new earth: and the former shall not be remembered, nor come into mind." **Revelation**

21:1 chimes in with these words. "And I saw a new heaven and a new earth: for the first heaven and the first earth were passed away;" And finally we see this written in God's word in **Revelation 21:4.** "And God shall wipe away all tears from their eyes; and there shall be no more death, neither sorrow, nor crying, neither shall there be any more pain: for the former things are passed away."

Here is the point. The devil knows what awaits us on the other side of this thing that we call life. He hates that God offers us what he himself can never again have, eternal life, peace, and contentment. In his rage he has launched an all-out attack against the character of God. He intensifies this attack when we are most vulnerable.

His goal is to have us to lose sight of a loving and compassionate God. Our God is doing everything in His Holy power to redeem and save us from this world of gross darkness. The Bible says that God is not willing that any should be lost.

When the devil whispers that God does not care, remember that the devil is a liar and the father of a lie. When he murmurs that God cannot be trusted, keep in mind that he is still a liar. When he comes directly after your life with the lie of all lies, "God can never forgive you." Know that there is no truth in him. God love is greater than our biggest sin.

What the devil has been after all along is your life. He deceitfully and repeatedly suggests what was mentioned earlier. "Life isn't worth living." "You'll be better off dead." "God doesn't care, nor does anyone else." "Why suffer like this when you can have perfect peace, when you can go to a place where no one can hurt you again, ever."

Contrary to the whisperings and outright boldface slanderous, slurs and smears of the devil, God is love. Everything about Him is good. Know that you can endure in the darkness, because of what God has done. Know that you can endure in the darkness, because greater is He that is in you than he that is in the world. Know that you can endure in the darkness, because Jesus is sincerely the light of the world just as you are His light in this world.

You must have the **AUDACITY to endure the darkness**, for it is but for a season. The light my friend is FOREVER! The darkness is only temporary.

Do not succumb to it. You are the children of light

who will be blessed to occupy the kingdom of light.

Revelation 22:5 confirms this truth with these

wonderful words. "And there shall be no night there;

and they need no candle, neither light of the sun; for

the Lord God giveth them light: and they shall

reign for ever and ever." Oh, dear fellow believers,

please endure the darkness with a bold **AUDACITY**.

The Good Shepherd is always nearby with the gifts

of love and eternity. The darkness is but temporary

experience for the children of light. Its time is limited,

but the light endures FOREVER. So right now,

please have the **AUDACITY** to endure the darkness.

What will you do when the darkness comes?

Will you trust God to get through it?

Will you let your light shine?

WELL, WILL YOU?

HAVE THE AUDACITY TO LIVE YOUR POWER

There is a story of a little dog named Jake. He had been abused and abandoned. He sat there with his big sad eyes in a cage fearfully trembling. On the very day that Jake would have been euthanized, a loving couple (Izzy and Lizzy) arrives looking for a family pet. The attendant in the shelter escorted the couple down the aisles of frightened animals. The attendant would make a few comments as she approached each cage. As they approached the aisle on which Jake was housed, they heard a little yelp. There he was, with his big sad eyes. He was as far back as he could get from the front door of the cage. He was just a little fellow. His ribs could be seen in his sides. He was visibly frightened and trembling as he curled himself into a ball trying to make himself smaller in an effort to be as inconspicuous as possible. The attendant began, "This is Jake. I do not think that he will make a very good pet. Something traumatic must have happened to him. He is not friendly or even approachable. I really do not think you would want this one." The attendant continued.

Izzy and Lizzy looked at Jake and then looked at each other as they both broadly smiled. "We will take Jake." They both said at the same time.

"Jake?" The attendant asked in disbelief.

"Absolutely." The couple asserted and smiled again. They carried little Jake home to their four-year-old son. A few years passed, and Jake had

Dr. J. Calvin Alberty

become an active, happy, and loving member of a warm, affectionate, and welcoming family.

In that cage, at the animal shelter, little Jake had no power. He was anxious and afraid. Perhaps, in his little young life he had been abused and traumatized. Jake needed just one thing. He needed love. However, he not only needed to be loved, but he also needed that love to be tangible and real. He needed it to be demonstrated in a way that he could sense and feel it. Fortunately, that is exactly what he got.

The love was experienced in the warm bath that he received when he arrived at his new home. The love was in the meals that he ate at regularly scheduled intervals. The love was in the special hugs that he received while sitting in the laps of his new family members. The love was in his fur being softly brushed, and the toy balls being thrown and tossed about. The love was especially felt by Jake in the home that was now his home. It was not just protection from the elements. The love that Jake most absorbed was the love he felt knowing that he was an intricate part of a special family.

Jake's power began manifesting itself in the wagging of his little stub of a tail, his running back and forth in a large, protected yard. Jake's power was evidenced as he challenged all visitors who rang the doorbell to identify themselves as friend or foe.

One night, when everyone was sound asleep, Jake smelled smoke. He began howling and barking.

He ran to Izzy and Lizzy's bedroom in a panicky state. His powerful barking woke them up in time to put out the fire. The shy little frightened pup who felt powerless, and whose life they had saved, was now returning the favor in a big way. Jake's heroics had saved Izzy and Lizzy's lives. This little, affectionate, and loving dog had the **AUDACITY** to find and live his power.

How about you? As a Christian, do you realize that God gave you power greater than Izzy and Lizzy were ever able to give to little Jake. Your power is real! The devil has gone back and forth throughout this world injuring Christians. They feel unloved and caged up in a state of fear like little Jake. Christ came to earth to rescue each of us. The devil has no power over a Christian.

When the enemy tries to claim a Christian, Christ sends angels that excel in strength. **Psalm 34:7** comforts us with these words. "The angel of the Lord encampeth round about them that fear him, and delivereth them." Like Jake with Izzy and Lizzy, when you become a part of the family of God, you are endowed with powers that are greater than anything that life or the devil can throw at you. **Matthew 10:1** says, "And when he had called unto him his twelve disciples, **he gave them power** against unclean spirits, to cast them out, and to heal all manner of sickness and all manner of disease." Each of us, as disciples of Christ are given power. **2 Timothy 1:7** states, "For God hath not given us the spirit of fear; **but of power**, and of love, and of a sound mind..."

Maybe you have been injured, wounded, or traumatized, if you have, you must believe that God knows exactly where it hurts. He knows your pain, your woundedness, your loss, your fear, your sadness, your sense of betrayal or being let down. God knows it all. Even deeper, God knows you. He knows the most intricate part of your soul. He knows every tear you have ever shed. He knows the sadness and desperation of your loneliest and darkest moments. God has given to you the power to overcome every challenge in your life. Whatever you do, you must never give up!

You are not alone. Christ Himself went through such an agonizing and harrowing ordeal. Remember, Jesus did not sense the presence of His Loving Father for what would be the darkest period of His life. This loneliness and abandonment had to be horrible and inconceivable of humans. We often read about Christ's death on the cross, but never really come close to comprehending its depth.

Jesus cried out to God His all-powerful Father, telling Him that He felt forsaken. This world will do that to all of us. It will cause us to feel forsaken and abandoned. Yet, we know that God was right there with Jesus. On the third day He arose and then ascended heavenward to be with His Father. Praise

God that his Loving Father accepted His great sacrifice.

Again, even though God was right there with Jesus, his presence could not be sensed. The darkness of our sins was upon Him. Our sins separated the Father and the Son for the first and only time in eternity. What a horrible experience this must have been for the Godhead.

Feeling abandoned has to be the same type or similar experience for us. In our darkest moments, when we cannot see Him, He is there! When we cannot feel Him, He is there! When we cannot hear Him, He is there! When we cannot find Him, He is there! He is not only there, but He is full of power. He gives and makes that power available to each believer when and wherever it is needed.

Love gave Jake the power to be the best little dog possible. He just needed that someone special in his life. God cries out to each of us. He begs us to let Him be that someone special in our lives. His love will make a difference. He will awaken the power in our lives in such a manner that we can become the greatest Kingdom-Builders ever. God's desire for you is that you will **"HAVE THE AUDACITY TO LIVE YOUR POWER!"**

Satan boasted about what he could to Job. Job was in a most pathetic condition. He had lost his children, his animals, his property, and was now covered over his entire body with the most painful type of sores and boils. His wayward friends made their way to him to question his loyalty and faithfulness to God. How lonely and abandoned poor Job must have felt. Yet we know from reading the book of Job that God was right there with him. God's attention never left him.

God's desire for you is for you to know that He is near, very near! He wants you know that He will never leave or forsake you. He has all power, and such power that He has He gives to you. Did you hear that? He gives it to you! It is His passionate desire that you will **"HAVE THE AUDACITY TO LIVE YOUR POWER!"**

God gave power to Izzy and Lizzy. Izzy and Lizzy gave that power to Jake and many others. It is so important that you survive the dark moments that test and challenge your soul. There are individuals in your future that you have not yet met. Yet, there is a day on God's divine calendar where they will enter your life-space. They are out there somewhere in the ether enduring conditions very much like Jake. God will bring them into your life so that you can share His amazing power with them. What am I saying to you? No, I should ask instead, what is God saying to us both?

Sometimes God allows us to go through ordeals that afflict us with great sorrows. We scream aloud, Lord help me. We cannot figure out why we must endure such a horrible ordeal. As you traverse through what appears to be your overwhelming experience, please think on this. Maybe God is allowing me to be prepared to help someone who will not survive without my help. Perhaps your pain is the result of God preparing you to be a healing aid to a sheep who would not survive without the medicine that God has placed in you.

I guess it is time for a little self-disclosure. I am a cancer survivor. My experience was extremely challenging. I am ashamed to say that I felt that sense of abandonment by God. I had professed that I would never ask Him "why me?" Yet there I was on what I thought was my death bed, when God, Who I could not sense, intervened to save my life.

A few years later, my eleven-year-old son would be diagnosed with terminal cancer. I had gone through a very rough ordeal in dealing with my own cancer, and now this. However, it was during that dark and isolated period of my life that I could see beautiful lights shining around me. After all, the stars can be seen best in the darkness of night. These stars brought me all types of natural herbal nutrition. I even acquired a Ph.D. in Wholistic Nutrition to try to help in remedying my condition.

I am earnestly pleading with you to listen to my words. It was in my darkest moment of life that God was giving me power. I was just like Jake. God was doing this wonderful miracle in ways unimaginable. He did not just do it for me, but this power spilled over into my son's life to restore health to his 11-year-old enfeebled body. It went further still to help others.

My greatest darkness would be my son's greatest light. This was orchestrated by our most loving and compassionate God. There is nothing that this sinful human being can take credit for, nor do I desire to take credit for any of God's great works. God did it all. I owe it all to God alone. The Good Shepherd was right there during all the times of my agony and pain. He was right there saving the life of both me and my son.

Whatever you are going through, please know in your heart that God is right there. He has been there all alone. Keep your eyes on the Good Shepherd. Stay close to Him and obey His every

command. Never forget that his love and power is
bigger than any problems that you might be
experiencing. Whatever He says is always for our
good. He admonishes us all to LIVE OUT YOUR
POWER!

Won't you live out the power that God has for you?

Will you receive the power that He has reserved

especially for YOU?

Will you share your power

with others to the Glory of

God?

WELL, WILL YOU?

THE AUDACITY OF THE PUREST POWER

The purest power of all is love. It has continuously been love. It will always be love. Be not deceived by the world around you. Wars, famines, riots, hate, prejudice, and everything else that is wrong with our world can be fixed by the power of love. I know that you have been told, and many others have been convinced, that such a simple answer is too simplistic and definitely unrealistic. They profess that such simplicity can never solve the problems enveloping earth. It is argued that the issues are too numerous, too complex, and too guarded by self-interest groups along party-lines that are riddled with greed.

However, I can with the utmost certainty assert that true godly love is enough to overcome the innumerable ills of humanity. I also have the absolute, unmitigated gall and **AUDACITY** to believe this to be true. I profess it without stuttering, hesitation, or qualifications. Love, and I mean real love, godly love can feed the hungry, shelter the homeless, comfort the fearful, convert the sinner, save the lost, and restore eons of lost faith in humanity.

The pure power of love is what hung Jesus on Calvary's cross. No man could have ever done that. Only love alone could do it. Now that is real power. Paul declared in **2 Corinthians 5:14** "For the love of Christ constraineth us…" Love is what brought God from heaven to be incarnated into a form called flesh. Love parted the Red Sea and called Lazarus from the grave. Love shut the mouths of lions. It made the fiery furnace powerless. It is because of love that we have the **AUDACITY** to profess a faith that cannot be conquered, bought, or squelched by the enemy.

Love is the purest of all powers, the strongest of all remedies, and the greatest of all forces known to humanity. It is the glue that holds every Christian together, the path that leads to a life, new and eternal. It is the source of everything of true value, and the only antibiotic to cure hate, racism, and prejudice. Tina Turner sang, "What's love got to do with it?" For the worshipers of Christ, it has everything to do with it, and everything to do with everything.

The enemy of souls desires desperately to destroy you, which equates to destroying your power. If he cannot destroy you or your power, then he will lead you through paths that are filled and muddled with wasted energy and time. You will find yourself roaming aimlessly down trails never meant for you.

The power that God has given to the church is insurmountable and insuperable. The devil cannot take it away, but what he can do is convince

Dr. J. Calvin Alberty

Christians who are feeling disregarded and marginalized that God's power is not meant for them. He can hide our power from us by keeping our attention focused elsewhere. Satan's goal is to have you to deny yourself access to that power given to you by God. In essence, he will have you to do what he cannot do. He knows that if he can get you to feel that "love is too soft or too frail" for the dark state of humanity's condition, you are on the verge of becoming prey.

He then moves you to an eye-for-an-eye mindset. This equates to the type of thinking that says we must get back at what came after us. We must meet evil with evil; force with force; or anger with greater anger. Now he has you right where he

244

wants you. He has you trying to do things in your own strength in a field far away from the Good Shepherd.

You are in a mode where you are unaware of your weakness and your powerlessness. However, Satan is very aware of your entrance into his killing field. You are placing your primal and feral self in a position to be ravaged by the devil. Your own strength as you will sadly discover, is no strength at all. While abandoning God's directives by standing in your own strength, or should I say weakness. You are prey.

Satan knows that if he can get you to put anything before the love of God and humanity, then you are already a breathing corpse. He knows that if you place self, jobs, family, friends, or your angry solutions for His solutions of love, you are at a great distance from the Good Shepherd. By doing so you are now in great danger of being devoured by wolves. When we reject the power that we find in God's love, we become food for wolves.

God's power of love can only be used to improve and heal the lives and lot of humanity. Jesus tells us to love our enemies. Only the power of love can do that. Jesus knows that if you consistently and sincerely love your enemy, that love will alter and bring that enemy into God's family of believers.

Love kills enemies and gives birth to new friends. This love is powerful. Jesus says turn the other cheek when offended by others. Only God's love can make that a reality. He even says in **Matthew 5:44** "But I say unto you, Love your enemies, bless them that curse you, do good to them that hate you, and pray for them which despitefully use you, and persecute you."

Only God's love can do that! You might ask, "How can love do that?" The answer is so remarkably simple. **God is love**. The Bible says that nothing is impossible with God. With this in mind, allow me to declare that there is nothing impossible with Love. It is the purest power. It is what unites heaven to earth. It is what reunited God to man. It is the inexplicable, unfathomable, and profound power of Pure Love. It will bring Jesus back to the earth for His second coming. It will raise the dead in Christ. It will transform the righteous living from mortality to immortality. It will forever do away with the sin problem, and there will be no more separation from our great God of love.

This is the essence of the purest power. Love is the game changer. It levels every playing field. It does what nothing else can do. There is no substitute or alternative for it. Every expression of real love comes from Christ. If you would allow me to paraphrase **1 Corinthians 13th** chapter, I would put it like this. "Without love we are nothing. We could give everything that we own to the poor, we could even sacrifice our bodies to the fire, but it would not mean a thing if it were not inspired by love. Love puts up with and tolerates a great deal of stuff. It does so in a kind and tender way. Love has no envy or pride

problems. It does not act strange or seek an

advantage over others. Love is not rash, nor is it

inspired by evil thoughts. Love rejoices in the truth.

When things would fall down or apart, love bears

them all and holds them together. Love believes all

things. It is full of hope that outlast everything. Love

never fails... We only know what God reveals to us

now in His prophetic word. However, when Jesus

returns, He will do away with our knowing only in

part. When we were children, we talked like children.

We understood as children, we thought as children,

but when we became adults, we put away childish

things. For now, we do not understand fully. We only

know in part; but when Jesus returns, we will know

even as we are known. At this moment, faith, hope, and love lives among us, these three. Hear well what I am telling you, when you consider them all, Love is the greatest thing that we have ever been privileged to experience.

The purest power is given to you.

Are you willing to receive it?

Will you let love in to alter your life forever?

WELL, WILL YOU?

THE AUDACITY OF THE RIDICULOUSNESS

Perhaps you might perceive it strange, that right after I tell you of the power of love, I would dare to articulate a ridiculous statement like "When we are weak, we are strong." Yet that is exactly what I have the **AUDACITY** to do. I would never make such a declaration to a world of carnality. However, to the believer, I make this claim without equivocation.

The sanity of this paradoxical or seemingly contradictory statement is in our understanding of "power and strength." The first part of this equation is, "God is our strength and our power. Apart from God, we can do nothing to defend ourselves. The darkness is too great for any mere mortal alone. The enemy is too cunning, the odds too overwhelming.

The darkness is too gross. Without God, I am nothing and can do nothing. It is in God that **Acts 17:28** affirms, "… we live, and move, and have our being." If we are anything, it is because of Christ. We owe everything to Him. **John 5:30**, reads, "I can of mine own self do nothing:" **John 15:5** makes this point even clearer. "I am the vine, ye are the branches: He that abideth in me, and I in him, the same bringeth forth much fruit: for **without me ye can do nothing**."

When we fully comprehend our own helplessness apart from Christ, we will be so desirous for his presence in every aspect of our lives. We will long for His peace and assurance. In fact, if we had just the smallest inkling of how desperately we need Him, we would be terrified of our Shepherd's absence.

It is only when we understand our true powerlessness, that we can appreciate His great and immense strength. Listen, when He wraps His love around us, He concomitantly wraps His power around us. There is a song entitled, "Just A Closer Walk With Thee" that begins, "I am weak but Thou art strong." If you listen to the meaning of these words, they profess, not so much a peace in our weakness as they do a peace in His love. His love is our strength.

When we consider this in light of the 23rd Psalm, it is even more comforting. Think on this portion and then think on it again. **Psalm 23:4** "Yea, though I walk through the valley of the shadow of death, I will fear no evil: for thou art with me; **thy rod and thy staff** they comfort me." The wolf and the lion are afraid of the shepherd's rod and staff, but not the sheep. The sheep know that these will only be used for guidance with them in a manner that keeps them safe. However, the wolves and the lions on the other hand, see the rod and staff as weapons that can in a brief moment end their lives.

God's love is power and peace to me and those of the Kingdom of Light. Yet, on the other hand, God's love is a weapon against the kingdom of darkness and all its minions. His wall of love keeps me within the realm of safety, but outside those walls, we see wolves and lions lurking with dastardly intents. The intentions of the wolves mean nothing to the Christians. Christians know that they are perfectly safe with the Good Shepherd. They also know that the wolves are utterly powerless to penetrate God's fortress of love.

Yes, I may be weak, but He is strong. He fights my battles, while I rest in peace, His peace. It is a peace that I do not understand, but it is one that I surely welcome. I am sure that this is that wonderful peace that Paul writes to the Philippians about when he says in **Philippians 4:7** "And the peace of God, which **passeth all understanding,** shall keep your hearts and minds through Christ Jesus." When we give everything to Jesus and stop lugging around our dark history of disappointments and failures, we become empowered. Satan repeatedly attempts to use the defeats and setbacks of our past lives to trouble and bother our spirit. We must know that beyond the devil's continued accusation is God's love. It is the same love that has been taking care of us for our entire lives. **1 Peter 5:7** teaches, "Casting all your care upon him; for he careth for you." Let go and let God.

Are you ready to cast your cares away? Do you desire His perfect peace? Then what are you waiting on? Give your mind, shoulders, back, and legs a rest. Start casting my brothers and sisters. START CASTING! Casting will prepare us by lightening our load for the arduous work ahead.

It is ridiculous to think that we can be strong in our weakness. It is ridiculous to think that God would become man. It is ridiculous that those He came to save would kill Him. It is ridiculous to think that a woman could have a baby without the help of a man. Even now, it is ridiculous to think that Jesus is willing to take all our pain and cares upon Himself. Unbelievers say that it is ridiculous to hope for what we cannot see. We appear ridiculous to most of the inhabitants of this earth. SO-WHAT? I assure you that a life with Christ is most wonderful and amazing.

Are you willing to appear ridiculous to unbeliever?

WELL, ARE YOU?

<u>So, You Thought That Heaven Would Be Easy?</u>

Who was it that had the **AUDACITY** to say that heaven would be easy? Only a clueless and naïve person with little life experience or even less time with God's word would have reached such a fairytale-like conclusion.

Athletes dedicate their all in their preparation for success in their athletic events. They assume nothing and work for everything. They give their all tirelessly with little or no mumbling or complaining. They seek to be the absolute best in their earthly pursuit to establish world records that document their outstanding and superior prowess. They know from the very beginning of their journey that it is going to be a tedious and difficult undertaking. They innately know within the deepest part of themselves, that everyone would be doing it if it was going to be easy. They are driven to **persist** by the burning desires of their **purpose** and **passion**. They strive for excellence at incomprehensible levels. The money, prestige, and/or prominence is a nice addition. However, excellence is their engine, and **purpose** and **passion** are their high-octane fuels that drive them to **persist**.

In the big picture, these athletes invest massive amounts of energy, time, and resources for what is but a temporary gain. If they can do this for so little (in the big scheme of things), then how much more should we, who seek things eternal, be dedicated to striving for our lofty and noble goals?

Additionally, not only are we striving to obtain something that is not bound by time or distance, but we are striving for the eternal good of others as well as ourselves.

It is a path and choice filled with tangibles and intangibles goals of empowerment and achievement. It is a sharing of power that will lead and guide others to our wonderful God. All glory to our God who is of perpetuity, infinity, and eternity. Our God is full of grace and love. Our God is forever alive to intercede and mediates on our behalf.

What we are striving for in our race is so incomprehensible that we cannot dare to imagine its depth and breadth, nor the enormity of what God has in store for those who love Him? Allow me to repeat

1 Corinthians 2:9 once again, "But as it is written, Eye hath not seen, nor ear heard, neither have entered into the heart of man, the things which God hath prepared for them that love him." How can anything be so amazing and so undeserved, and yet God has prepared it as a reward for the very humanity that murdered His Only Begotten Son. With such a reprehensible behavior on our part toward our God, how could we still somehow think that obtaining heaven would be easy. The "going home with Jesus" part is not the difficult task. It is getting ourselves out of God's way with all our foolishness about working to earn salvation.   We do not work to be saved. We work because we are saved. Our salvation is by grace and mercy. Grace is God giving us what we do not deserve. These would be things such as salvation and eternal life. Mercy on the other hand, is God withholding from us what we do deserve. These would be things like eternal death and hopelessness. Even with grace and mercy, this life is at times exceedingly difficult.

James Cleveland sang a line in a song that said, "Nobody told me the road would be easy." Allow me to confirm, the road is not easy, though there are some particularly good days and times.

On other days, every single step is a challenge. Sometimes even getting out of bed is difficult. Over-filled hospitals and graveyards attest to life's difficulties. If we, as created beings of the Living God, would follow the true Shepherd our lives would be so much better. If we listen to **His** voice only, and pursue only the true Shepherd, Leader, Provider, and Defender, our lives would be better. We must avoid these pretenders, who I like to call false prophets. If we would but do these few things, we would be immensely better prepared to lead flocks of thirsting souls to Christ.

If the church is not producing good leaders, then perhaps this is the case because it has moved too far from the true leader. As Jesus said to his mother and earthly father, "Didn't you know that I would be about my Father's business?" We too, MUST ever be in the mode of being about our Father's business. This is a posture that we must assume now and continually. It is hard being a

Dr. J. Calvin Alberty

Christian. The road to heaven is hard. It is narrow
and filled with all types of pitfalls. Matthew warns us
in **Matthew 7:13-14**, "Enter ye in at the strait gate: for
wide is the gate, and broad is the way, that leadeth
to destruction, and many there be which go in
thereat: Because strait is the gate, and **narrow** is the
way, which leadeth unto life, and **few** there be that
find it."

 With all its challenges, with all its trials and
tests, God still declares that we must face the
adversities of life with a boldness that is based on
our trust of Him. We dare not faint in the face of such
adversities. We must be strong in God's strength
when life gets hard, and then even harder. We must
not compromise with this world, no matter the

hurdles before us. We must be inconsolable apart from God. Nothing on this earth should comfort us when it removes us from His presence, principals, or providential love. When thing just seem overwhelming and impossible, remember that there is nothing too hard for God. Yes, there is definitely a liability in following God in a world that hates Him and you. However, these liabilities are reconciled to this world only. The most eternal and damning liability ever, is to follow Satan anywhere, for any reason, and for any amount of time.

No, I cannot tell you that heaven is easy. I cannot tell you that it is cheap. I cannot tell you that it will not call for you to sacrifice everything. Yet, what I can tell you, is that no matter how much it costs, or demands on our parts for sacrifice and obedience, all I can tell you is that heaven is worth it.

Do you have the **AUDACITY** to tell this world that loving Jesus with all your heart, requires that all your heart be surrendered to Him? Are you prepared to journey the narrow and hard road to heaven? Are you prepared to face adversities and suffer persecution and oppression for your faith in God?

Do you have the **AUDACITY** to do that?

Do you have the **AUDACITY** to be a Christian?

WELL, DO YOU?

www.ingramcontent.com/pod-product-compliance
Lightning Source LLC
Chambersburg PA
CBHW060537260626
47161CB00003B/943